UNDER THE DARK
WATER

ISBN 978-0-9929202-9-6

Copyright © Roy Eynhallow
and Hallow Books 2016

This book is dedicated

*To my wonderful wife
without whom this book
would not have seen the light of day.
Thank you for motivating me along the way.*

*To my parents who have given me
amazing educational opportunities.
Mum, Dad, thank you for making me work hard
and for supporting my choices.*

Thank You!

In the beginning of the book, I would like to thank the people who have contributed to the creation of this book.

I would like thank every teacher whom I have met in my life. Thank you for challenging me, for making me notice my own mistakes and teaching me how to correct them. I am especially grateful to all my English teachers. Thank you for making me see the beauty of the English language and for helping me discover that special way to look at every word as if I see it for the first time.

I would also like to thank Jane Harry and Peter Shortall who edited and proofread this book. Thank you for correcting all my mistakes. And, of course, last but not least, I would like to thank my main editor – Luciana Sabina Tcaciuc, my wife.

Table of Contents

Part One: April – May

Chapter 1: Mark	1
Chapter 2: Sarah	6
Chapter 3: Mark	8
Chapter 4: Sarah	19
Chapter 5: George	30
Chapter 6: Mark	34
Chapter 7: Mark	39
Chapter 8: Sarah	54
Chapter 9: George	65
Chapter 10: George	68
Chapter 11: Mark	72

Part Two: June – July

Chapter 12: George	91
Chapter 13: Mark	97
Chapter 14: Sarah	107
Chapter 15: George	114
Chapter 16: Sarah	125
Chapter 17: George	129
Chapter 18: Mark	135
Chapter 19: Mark	140

Chapter 20: George	149
Chapter 21: Mark	158
Chapter 22: Sarah	171
Chapter 23: Mark	182

Part Three: August – September

Chapter 24: Sarah	197
Chapter 25: Mark	202
Chapter 26: George	212
Chapter 27: Sarah	220
Chapter 28: Mark	226
Chapter 29: Mark	231
Chapter 30: Sarah	235
Chapter 31: Mark	240
Chapter 32: Sarah	248
Chapter 33: Mark	252
Chapter 34: Mark	263
Chapter 35: Epilogue	271
About the Author	273

Part One

April – May

Chapter 1

Mark

Mark Davies was sitting on his bed. Downstairs, his parents were arguing.

'You bloody scoundrel! Look at yourself now! No, you just bloody look at yourself,' Mark heard his mother say. It wasn't the first time she had spoken in this tone, but it still cut across his ears. He hated to hear his parents argue – and recently he had heard more of it than ever before.

'You come home god knows when, completely legless, stinking of beer! It's the same every evening. You can't even imagine how tired I am!'

Join the club, Mum, Mark thought bitterly. He didn't even have to be eavesdropping to hear the voices from downstairs. He heard the heavy footsteps of his father as he stumbled across the kitchen floor. His mother was right, though – he had to witness this sort of dialogue far too often… and he was getting angrier each time. There was no one he could talk to about it, either. His anger was boiling inside him and Mark feared that at some point the tiniest trigger would make him explode. Already he was walking home and his fists were itching to punch something or someone. *Just give me a reason,* he thought over and over. *Just try picking on me, anyone, and you'll be swallowing your teeth ...*

But there was nothing to set him off, and the darkening cloud kept rumbling inside him, with no space to trigger lightning and set the thunder rolling.

'Listen, Sarah, and listen carefully,' his father's voice boomed back. 'I am a hard-working man and if I wanna visit the pub after work, I will go there and have my time with my mates. No one can stop me.'

'Wh-what mates, George?' Mark's mother said, her voice shaky with that forced, tart laughter. 'What mates? Those winos reeking of drink and piss? You know too well how much money we've got and you spend it on something that will end up as puke and piss in the Railway-bleeding-Inn!'

'You ain't making me feel guilty for wanting to relax. I have a right to that!'

'To relax? To *relax*?' Mark could almost see his mother's face – and the way sarcasm changed all her features. 'Then tell me – when will *I* have a right to relax? When was the last time we went out together as a family? I can see it in Mark: he's retreating into himself.'

'It's perfectly normal for his age,' Mark's father retorted.

Good one, Dad, Mark thought. *Indeed, it's perfectly normal to want to smash someone's face in every day when you're fourteen.*

'It's not normal for me,' he heard his mother say. 'We hardly ever talk lately. Oh, I can't understand why

I'm explaining all of this to you,' she snapped all of a sudden. 'You're drunk and won't remember anything tomorrow morning! Don't you get it? You don't even have the health to drink like your mates do!'

This was true – and Mark's father knew it. The voices downstairs fell silent for a moment; Mark thought that his father was probably digesting what his mother had just said to him. Yes, he knew he did not have the health… it was just that he didn't like being reminded of it. Nobody knew where he'd picked up the idea, but George Davies considered being infirm in any way a personal insult to his dignity. He would not want to hear about doctors, medicine, or having restrictions in food, drink or activities.

Still, dignity or no dignity, a stomach ulcer was a stomach ulcer, with all the unpleasant consequences – and he had to learn to live with it. Instead, he chose denial.

It was Mark's mother that broke the silence.

'Look at me, George!' she said. 'Look at my face if you can still see something – look at the wrinkles all over my face! I'm freakin' thirty-eight and that's how I look.'

'You ain't making me guilty of making you look one way or another! It's none of my fault, and you stop nagging me for that. A lady should look after herself and it's not the man's duty to make her do it. All my mates like a drink and I'm no different from them – and none of their wives scream at them like you do.'

Upstairs, Mark jumped off his bed, flung his jacket on, pulled on his trainers and grabbed the door handle.

He couldn't stay in the house any more – if he did, he would surely break something in his room. The walls seemed to advance onto him and the April evening was stuffy and uncomfortably warm, despite the open window. As he descended the stairs, the fitted carpet on them concealed his footsteps – but his parents were so engrossed in the argument that they would not hear him even if he were stomping.

'Well, that makes me the only sane woman in the entire city, then,' he heard his mother say. 'Besides, perhaps if you made me scream more at night, I would scream less during the day!'

Mark froze on the middle of the staircase – but not because of what his mother had just said. From his position on the stairs, he could see both his parents in the kitchen, facing one another…

And there was *a third one*.

Mark's stomach turned to icy liquid and, for a split second, his anger gave way to terror.

Mark had seen one of *them* before but he knew he would never get used to them. He hoped he was just imagining *it*, yet *it* was standing before him and staring at him, unblinkingly, as real as anything. A pale figure in white overalls, like the ones workers wear…

And it had a horse's head.

The hooves of the creature were extended and looked almost like hands, except that he could discern no fingers. It seemed that the creature was wearing black gloves that glistened as if they were made of some slimy leather.

Mark looked into its unblinking eyes, the two blotches of dark, oily shoe polish – and then, in a blink of an eye, the vision disappeared. It must have lasted no more than a second. Mark's foot landed onto the next step when, as if through some haze, he heard his mother say:

'If you're such a hard-working man in the pub with your mates, then why can't you work harder with me?'

Then he heard a dull slap and a sharp intake of breath. Two seconds of hazy silence followed.

'You… hit me,' his mother said. There was no surprise in her voice, no anger… there was no emotion he could name.

'You hit me,' she repeated. Mark saw his father standing dejectedly in the kitchen, his arms hanging limply at his sides.

Mark should have stayed. But the thoughts about the argument and the vile creature with a horse's head pushed him out of the house and he could bear it no longer. He jumped down the stairs with a crashing thud, rushed outside and slammed the door. He should have stayed and done something, but he didn't know what to do. He just left.

As he was shutting the door after himself, he heard his mother's first sob.

Chapter 2

Sarah

Sarah Davies shut herself in a spare room and lay on the mattress that was placed directly on the floor – the room did not have a bed because they never needed one there. Next, she covered herself with a prickly woollen blanket and cried.

She knew it was no use talking to George now – he was a lightweight although he would never admit to it, and whatever he had drunk would make him fall asleep soon. Tomorrow, he wouldn't remember anything she'd say now. Sarah had never felt so old and tired. And helpless.

She could not believe that George had hit her. In sixteen years of marriage, he had never laid a finger on her. On second thoughts, she had provoked him, but she was simply sick and tired of his drinking. Yet, it was the death of his sister that pushed him to drink... Sarah was sick and tired of finding excuses, too.

Of course she would try to forgive him because she believed this wasn't him. He was not being himself. And this was shy she was so upset... Drinking for six months was beyond grief. It was a problem. Sarah could not shake off the nagging feeling that unless she stopped it, it would tear her family apart. Her family that she had made such an effort to create and maintain.

And Mark... she knew why he left. It wasn't very nice of him to slam the door and just walk out without a word, but it was a gesture. If she were him, she would have probably walked out too. When George had drunk in the past, he had never been violent and he had known his limits; he would seem totally removed from the world – silent and aloof, lost somewhere in the endless passages of his thoughts. She was familiar with this state of his, and was used to it. But the violent George seemed strange, unpredictable and scary.

There must be a way, she thought. She must stop her husband from drinking, somehow.

Sarah cried herself to sleep. Her last thought before she fell asleep was about her son, Mark.

She woke up two hours later when she heard him unlocking the door. She decided not to tell him anything or ask any questions; she just wanted to make sure he was okay and send him to bed.

Chapter 3

Mark

Mark was striding down a badly lit street, clenching his fists in the pockets of his jacket. He was not looking where he was going and almost bumped into a low-hanging street sign. For a moment, he stared at the green paint on the metal. Then he drew back his fist and slammed it into the sign, leaving knuckle prints on the even surface. The sign rang loudly in protest. Mark rubbed his knuckles. Damn, that hurt!

He entered a large park by the canal. There was sweat on his face, which he wiped off with a sleeve – it was a hot day. Perhaps it was too warm for the jacket, or maybe it was the unusual heat of the day that the gathering clouds had kept close to the ground. They were also making the evening look darker than it actually was. On a normal day Mark would go to the canal – when in the evening you looked into its dark waters at a certain angle you could see the industrial lights being reflected. At the moment, Mark hated the heat, the lights and the glistening black water. He headed to the furthest end of the park – the place where he was almost sure he would be undisturbed. Away from the canal, away from the joggers… His head was exploding and he needed to think about too many things. He wanted to do it alone.

Mark reached a wooden bench at the furthest end of the park, kicked it – the wood answered with a dry thud – and then slumped onto the boards.

'Damn you all. Go screw yourselves, all of you!' he hissed and spat on the ground. Then he shut up, realising he was talking to himself, and looked around. There was no one to watch him; he slouched back in the curve of the bench and peered into his own trainers.

All the days had become the same. He stayed at home and heard endless arguments that had stolen not only his mother's peace, but also his. He knew the reason why his father drank… but how could he even try to understand him? How do you try to understand the man who can only see the world through the bottom of the glass? It had been going on for over five months, since that accident when Aunt Celia… Mark was not present then, but he could not bear to think about it, and he wouldn't wish anyone to witness it.

And he had a secret. Something that he could never share with anyone. He could see something that others could not.

What were these… *creatures*? Could you even call them 'creatures'? This would imply they have been *created*. Who in their right mind could create these beings?

Why did he see them? *What* did he see, if anything?

In his mind, in his dreams – and sometimes even in his living room – the blotches of black oil stared at him from the pale, repulsive horse's head. He had started seeing them since his father started drinking. But it was not the first time. He had a feeling of having seen this head, these white overalls, the slick black gloves and boots before... as if some elements of his childhood nightmares had come together and blended into that grotesque figure. Childhood nightmares that woke him crying before he could speak. Were such memories even possible?

Mark buried his face in his hands and ran his fingers through his hair, ruffling it. Sweat made it stay up – the stuffy warmth was not abating. What on earth was happening to him? Was he going bonkers or what? His own family were driving him mad.

'God, I hate my family,' he said aloud. 'Nothing but a bunch of problems!'

'Excuse me?' a voice sounded above his head. A girl's voice, but low, slightly guttural, as if from frequent shouting – almost like a boy's.

'Huh?' Mark lifted his head and looked up. There was a girl standing in front of him. He looked at her in surprise: amid the stuffiness of the evening, she emitted freshness. Her dark skin stood out against her grey jersey tracksuit that looked fresh and clean. Mark's nostrils caught a faint smell of fabric softener. She was holding a strange device in her hand – something like a long plastic ladle: a handle with a round-bottomed cup at the end. There was a tennis ball sitting tightly in the cup.

'Have you seen a dog run nearby?' the girl asked. 'It's a black Labrador retriever.'

'No.' The answer came before Mark could think about the rules of politeness. 'Sorry, I haven't,' he added after a short pause.

'You haven't, have you? All right then,' the girl said. 'And by the way,' she added, 'what a horrible thing to say. How can you talk about your family like that?'

'It's none of your business.' Again, the answer came before he could restrain himself. The dark cloud was rumbling ever louder and the first lightning was ready to flash. Now he wanted to step out of line as much as he could allow himself. 'And by the way,' he added, mocking her. 'Eavesdropping is bad for your health. Do it to the wrong person, and you might end up with a black eye.'

To his surprise, the girl giggled.

'Ah tink dey ah black enough aw-ready, doncha tink?' The last words were said in a thick mock-Jamaican accent. This was certainly not the reaction Mark was expecting. He just wanted her to get offended and walk away. He listened to her laughter and exhaled heavily.

'Yeah, right,' he uttered, not knowing what else to say.

'So you've not seen him, have you?' the girl repeated. Mark shook his head.

'Where could he have gone?' the girl said to herself, rubbing her chin. 'Spot! Spot!' she shouted suddenly to the left and to the right, walking away from him.

The girl's giggles were still echoing in Mark's head when a thought struck him. Call a dog? He knew a better way than to shout.

'Hey, look here!' he said to the girl, rummaging through his jacket pockets. The girl stopped at his voice and looked back. Mark pulled a shiny metal object, a small tube, no longer than a pinkie finger, from his pocket. He had recently traded his slingshot for it. The boy who gave it to him said it emitted sounds that only animals could hear – but he hadn't had a chance to try it out yet.

'I've got, like, this whistle here,' Mark said. 'It's meant to attract dogs. Shall I try it? Maybe he'll come.'

'Go on,' the girl said. To Mark's surprise, there was a challenge in her voice. Mark put the whistle to his lips and blew sharply. A high-pitched sound emerged and hung in the air, blending with the sounds of the church bell, as the clock struck half past nine.

Suddenly, enthusiastic barking could be heard from afar; the barking grew louder and, seconds later, a black dog flew out of the bushes, panting, with its tongue hanging out. The whistle had worked – Mark was glad about it. It was a good slingshot with a carved handle – he'd made it himself.

'Spot, you little bugger!' the girl exclaimed, grabbing the dog by the collar and wrestling it down by tugging on its ears. 'Where've you been? You're all scruffy – how did you even manage to find so much dirt to stick onto yourself? You're such a pig!'

The dog looked scruffy indeed – half of its body was wet, showing that it had been taking an illegal dip in the pond, and there was mud and silt on its coat. A burdock burr was stuck behind its left ear. It looked happy as a child who had been playing in a puddle.

The girl stopped tugging the dog's large, long ears (did they look this way because she had been pulling them since the dog was a pup, Mark wondered) and rose to her feet, facing him.

'Thank you,' she said with a smile. 'I like that whistle of yours – a nice thing to have,' she added.

Mark looked at the girl again. She cocked her head and looked back at him. He wanted to say something to her – and somehow he guessed that she knew it. What was more, she invited him to say it.

'You know what?' he uttered finally. 'You're tough.'

'What d'you mean?'

'Well, I've been rude to you, and you don't seem to give a damn.'

The girl smiled in response. Her eyes wandered towards the dog that was impatiently pacing around, not too far from them, and then back to Mark. It was this smile, simple and careless, that made Mark remember what he'd said to her and brought some colour to his face. 'Sorry,' he said, lowering his eyes.

'My dad said to me once that if someone calls you an idiot and you get offended, it means you *are* an idiot.'

'Yeah, right,' Mark said. 'Next you're going to tell me that you don't ever get annoyed by anything, then you'll, like, graciously spread your white wings and take off into the blue yonder.'

To his surprise, the girl laughed again.

'And what about my dog? I'm not going anywhere without him.'

Mark had an answer for that:

'Why, he can flap his ears. It might do something – considering that his grandma probably had an affair with a basset-hound…'

The girl bent towards her dog again and lifted its large floppy ears.

'Nice one,' she said. 'I've never thought about that – but he's got rather large ears for a Lab.' Then she straightened up and extended her hand to Mark.

'I'm Tandi, by the way.'

Mark shook her hand and said his name. 'How often does he run away?' he asked, nodding at the dog.

'Spot? Quite a bit actually. But he comes back shortly after. I trust him – he wouldn't go for good. But he likes sticking his nose where he shouldn't – abandoned buildings and rubbish dumps. Once he ran away and didn't show up for two days.'

'Bit like I'm going to,' Mark said.

'What?' Tandi asked.

Run away. He had been considering this option for some time. He was so tired of hearing nothing but arguments all the time – perhaps if he disappeared for some time, his parents would unite to search for him? He didn't know what had pushed him to say his next words – but, for some reason, he felt safe voicing his thoughts in front of this girl, Tandi.

'I'm gonna run away,' he repeated. 'Had enough at home. No one's paying any attention to me, anyway.'

Once again, the girl's reaction was not what he was expecting.

'Oh, really?' she said, cocking her head. 'Or are you telling me this because you want to impress me?'

'Why would I want to impress you?' Mark said, indifferently. 'It's happening and that's that. If you don't believe me, I'll do it out of spite.'

What was this girl playing at? Did she really view his actions only as a way of making her interested in him? Well, she could think whatever she wanted – he didn't have the slightest inclination to do so.

'You're talking like you know me inside-out,' Mark said, irony back in his voice.

'Why do you want to flee anyway?'

'Flee? That's not what I want. More like distance myself, perhaps.'

'Oh, keep your poetry for English classes,' Tandi cut him off. '*Why*, Mark?'

Before he knew it, the words just came pouring out of his mouth.

''Cause I'm fed up,' he said. 'There's nothing but crap at home. My father started drinking and my parents are constantly arguing. I've had enough.'

'You think you're the only one with problems?' Tandi asked.

'Everyone's got problems. But from my perspective, mine are the biggest,' Mark retorted.

'And where are you going to live?' she asked, ignoring his last remark.

Mark hadn't given it much thought. But he would never admit to it.

'I've got some... places sorted out for the short term. And then, it's April. I'd hitch a ride down south, to Devon for the summer.'

'I don't think you have a plan,' Tandi said. 'If you run away, you'll come back after two days or so. That, or rain, wind and mud – being a tramp is harder than you think. But you won't run away in the first place. Wanna know why?'

'Go on?' Despite himself, Mark became interested. What would this girl say to stop him from doing what he wanted?

'Because you'll meet me here, at this very bench, this Saturday at 2 o'clock. And I mean it. Come on, Spot!' Tandi called and strode away, the black Labrador following closely at her heels, wagging its tail. He watched her grey jersey tracksuit blend with the greenery of the park, until she disappeared.

Mark blinked and stared at the trees where the girl had just been. What had just happened? Did she just tell him to meet her? A total stranger. What was that supposed to mean? It sounded almost like... like she had invited him on a date in a very strange way.

A date was the last thing he had expected, or in fact needed. The events of the evening were spinning at the back of Mark's mind. His parents arguing. *His father hit his mother.* It was the first time that had happened. And the *thing* he, Mark, saw in the kitchen while standing on the stairs. He was sure neither of his parents had seen it. So, had he really seen it, or was he just going bonkers? Would he be like their strange neighbour, old Oak, soon?

What a crazy evening! All of this and then this Tandi…

Wait a minute!

As soon as Mark thought about the strange girl and her dog, he noticed that something had changed in his inner state. He thought of the way he felt… he was no longer angry. Instead, all of a sudden, exhaustion flushed over him like the last wave of warm wind; the temperature in the park dropped. Every muscle in his body felt heavy and inert as if filled with some viscous liquid.

Because you'll meet me here, at this very bench, this Saturday at 2 o'clock.

This was what she had said. This Saturday! It was in two days' time! Mark's brain refused to process any more information; all he wanted was sleep. It took double the usual effort to rise from the bench and walk home.

His father had gone to bed by the time he returned. His mother came out to meet him but he'd expected her to be more cross with him. He didn't remember much of what she said to him as he returned

– as if through the haze, he answered he was not hungry but very tired.

As soon as his head touched the pillow, the first lightning cracked the sky open and raindrops started beating on the roof like a million mad drummers.

Chapter 4

Sarah

The Birmingham market was as noisy as always. Traders with thick countryside accents were screaming their lungs out: 'Fruit and veg, ladies – any bowl a pound!', 'Buy fresh country eggs, two dozen in a box!', 'Rich English cheese, anybody?'

The voices were booming across the market square. Sarah was walking between the aisles, feeling slightly giddy because of all the smells and noises. It was good to go shopping in the morning – having some weekdays off was one of the advantages of working part-time as a secretary in an office.

Sometimes Sarah thought she would like to work full-time, to earn more. Yet, it had been hard to keep on top of things recently. If she had a full-time job, she would probably spend all the extra money on restoring lost health…

But even before George had started drinking, he had told her that she didn't need to work more than she was already. After all, he was earning enough. Yes, *was*. That was the key word. Recently he had been spending more and more time and money at the pub.

She could not believe that George had slapped her the night before. Over the entire course of their marriage, many things had happened. They did quarrel, but then, which couple did not? But George had never done so much as clench his fists at her – he was a simple man, no airs and graces about him, but he had always had a high degree of self-restraint. Was it the drinking that was doing it to him – taking over his life, pulling him away from the family and the real world?

'Hello, madam, anything from the counter?'

The trader's voice ripped her out of the world of her thoughts and jerked her back to the present. She raised her eyes at him, feeling startled and stupid.

'Anything from here, madam?' the man repeated, gesturing towards the range of dairy produce on his counter. Sarah stopped – but not because she was interested in buying anything. All of a sudden, a pang of pain shot through her stomach and the world went dark for a moment.

'Hey, madam, are you feeling all right?' the trader boomed. Sarah raised her eyes to look at the man's concerned face, but before she could answer anything, the world spun around her, she felt her knees give way and this time the darkness lasted longer.

*

Sarah's eyelids shot up when someone splashed water in her face. She woke up to find herself on the ground, with at least twenty people's faces surrounding her.

'What... what happened?' she asked, surprised at the weakness in her voice.

'You've fainted, my dear, that's what's happened,' a woman said to her left. 'This here butcher had to splash three glasses on you before you came round!'

Sarah felt a pair of strong hands hoist her up and put her back on her unsteady feet.

'You all right, love?' the man who lifted her asked. 'Not going to fall when I let go?'

Another man extended a glass of water towards her. Sarah drained the glass and tried to stand on her feet again.

'I'm fine, thank you,' she answered, putting strength into her voice. 'I'm fine,' she repeated, wiping her face with her sleeve. She brushed some of the water off her soaked jacket, and started walking away.

'Oh, no, you're not,' another voice said behind her and the woman felt a firm grip on her elbow. She spun around and breathed a sigh of relief.

'Mrs Blake,' she exhaled with a smile. 'I didn't see you.'

'There wasn't much you could see, you passed out, love!' Mrs Blake said. 'And call me Jo, I thought we'd agreed upon that.'

Jo Blake, a pleasant half-Irish, half-Scouse woman, was Mark's science teacher. Sarah was particularly happy to see her. She was a pleasant, homely lady who always wore home-knitted cardigans (she was really good at knitting and it was often impossible to tell that they were home-knitted) and did everything with a smile on her face. Sarah found her Northern humour particularly warm and welcoming.

'I still can't get used to it,' Sarah said, apologetically. 'You're my son's teacher after all…'

'Well, this is not school, and we're not exactly in a teacher-parent meeting,' Jo said. 'And don't steer the conversation the wrong way, love. I said you weren't alright, and there's no point wasting your breath telling me the opposite. You are coming to my place this instant. I live close by, as you remember.'

Sarah wanted to protest, but felt too weak to do even that. Jo fetched her bags and led Sarah away from the market, almost dragging her behind herself. Sarah dumbly followed, seeing everything as if through the haze. She only truly came to her senses when Jo placed a tray laden with pieces of chocolate brownie on the table and pushed a steaming mug of spicy-smelling tea into her hand.

'Thank you, Jo,' Sarah said, sinking into the chair and taking a sip.

'That's better,' Jo said, her face full of concern. 'I feel so old when people call me Mrs Blake. Besides, our conversations are about more than just school business, aren't they? We've known each other for over a year now. And I tell you what – when I first met you at the school, I immediately saw that you're a lovely woman,' she said, pushing a tray of biscuits towards Sarah. 'Mrs Davies,' she added pointedly.

Sarah laughed weakly.

'I get your point,' she said. Then, looking down into her own mug, Sarah saw that she'd drained her tea down to the last drop. She hadn't even noticed. She set the mug on the table.

'Here, have some more, my dear,' Jo encouraged her, refilling her mug. 'You look weak.'

'I feel weak,' Sarah replied. 'I needed to talk to you about it. I feel I'm losing my energy.'

'You can tell me anything, you know that.'

That was true. Sarah and Jo had become close friends since they first met during a teacher-parent meeting over a year earlier. It started after Sarah saw Jo's dress and complimented her on it. Jo told her that she'd had it tailor-made and was thinking of getting more. The two women started talking about sewing and knitting and Sarah told Jo she was skilled with a needle. Jo wanted Sarah to make some clothes for her and this was how their friendship began.

This kind woman with greying hair and a slight Northern twang in her otherwise perfect Received Pronunciation was the person to whom Sarah felt she could confide her secrets, just as she had been able to confide them to her husband until recently. Still, Sarah felt strange about their friendship. She had heard that girls and women usually pour their hearts out to one another – but she had never had the chance to experience this herself. She was an orphanage girl who started a family of her own after never having one. The orphanage had taught her to keep herself to herself, not to share her life with anyone, and even now, when she had Jo to talk to, she did not feel like telling everything at once. She knew – theoretically – that she could, but she hadn't actually shared anything too personal with her until then. It was a strange feeling – well, maybe not so strange to Sarah – she found comfort in the mere fact that Jo existed in her life. Talking was secondary, but having someone to talk to was paramount. Sometimes she still felt like a little orphanage girl who held the words inside herself, like balloons on a string.

Still, now it was time to let go of the strings.

'It's Mark…' she said, 'and my husband, too.'

She paused, and Jo nodded, encouraging her to continue.

'I'm worried about Mark. He's been really… reluctant to open up lately. He's being very difficult at home. I don't even want to know what he's like at school.'

Jo hesitated for a moment and then said:

'Well, he's not much trouble, to be fair… but he's been missing classes.'

Sarah sighed. It was just as she had thought.

'He's been keeping a low profile, though – and being very much aloof, I must say. Other teachers have reported that as well. But I don't think he'll get into trouble or fall in with a bad crowd if that's what you're worried about.'

Sarah took a large sip out of her mug. Jo talked about her fears as if she knew exactly what was troubling her. Even though she did not reveal too many details, this woman felt her, she really did. This made Sarah feel reassured.

'What worries me more, though,' the teacher continued, 'is that your son has hardly any company at all, bad or otherwise.'

'It's not surprising. Nor are his absences – I don't see much of him at home, either. That's why I'm worried.'

'Your son is fourteen now, am I right?' Jo asked.

'Almost fifteen,' Sarah said.

'It's a difficult age for him. Kids do close up at that age – I know, I've raised three children all by myself. They turned out all right.'

'As long as he keeps out of trouble...' Sarah said. 'You know, I haven't been able to talk to him properly in recent weeks.' She didn't know where she got this obsession from, but she did not like her son's silence at all. In her own teenage years, silence and aloofness had been her best friends and allies – but Mark was not her. He was not like her. He was angrier, voiced his frustration more openly. And yet, recently he'd been trying to hide it, to bottle it all up. She was glad that his bedroom door did not have a lock on it. She couldn't bring herself to think of the possibility of him doing something stupid.

'George and I had an argument yesterday,' Sarah said. She suddenly realised that she'd spent a lot of time in silence, thinking about what had been happening recently. 'He came home drunk, and I challenged him. We said some nasty words to each other, and then he slapped me. I think Mark heard us. He just slammed the door and left home without a word. I still don't know where he went. I didn't go to bed with George that night, I slept in the spare room. Mark came home rather late. I was tired and didn't ask him where he'd been. I just fear that he'll start taking drugs or even worse...' Sarah's voice became a whisper. She sipped more tea, feeling the hot liquid run down her throat and smoothen her voice. As she talked about it, she felt that the heavy feeling in her chest and stomach was subsiding.

'I don't know him that well,' Jo replied, 'but judging by what I know and what other teachers say, Mark is smart enough to stay out of trouble. Still, whatever is happening at home affects his behaviour at school. He's not the truant type. But when he is there, he stops participating in classes. It's not like he's struggling, either: he does know something, and makes an effort, too... but not enough, especially lately,' she concluded with a sigh.

'He's like that,' Sarah said. 'He studies when he chooses to...' Sarah mustered her courage before she said what she was going to. 'It's my husband, George. He's been spending too much time at the pub over the last five or six months. It started when...' the memory of that day came to her. She was there, saw the entire thing happen. 'His sister died in a car accident, Jo.' Sarah's voice started and stopped, dropping to a hoarse whisper as a sob got stuck in her throat. 'His sister was crossing the road. George waved at her, beckoning her to cross, when a car came speeding around the corner. You could've smelt the driver's breath a mile away...' She cut off, unable to continue. Ashamed of the tears dripping onto her lap and into her tea, she wiped them off.

'After that, George sort of...snapped. He drinks almost every day – and way more than he can handle. He's got a stomach ulcer... and he's had alcohol problems before. It was when his mother died. Except that last time he realised what was happening to him, he wanted to stop. Mark was only two back then. He doesn't remember. But now...'

Sarah gripped the cooling mug tightly to stop her hands from shaking.

'You want to help him, Sarah.' This was not a question. Not really a statement, either. Rather like a reminder of what she had to do, but didn't know how.

'I do, Jo. But I'm so tired and frustrated. George doesn't seem to want to help himself. Alcohol clouds his mind, he doesn't know what he's talking about. I'm scared for him. There's nothing I haven't tried: talking to him, pleading, shaming him, trying to frighten him... Now I can only shout at him. I'm trying to hurt his masculine pride – tell him he will become impotent. Maybe then he will think about what drinking is doing to him?'

Jo listened to Sarah's monologue patiently. When the woman lifted her eyes to look at the teacher, she saw attention and concentration in her face. Then Jo took Sarah's hand between her palms.

'One never knows how to react when things like that happen,' the teacher said. 'But I will tell you this:

there are better ways to show your husband that he's a man.'

Sarah shrugged.

'How? I'm tired, too tired.'

'I can see that,' Jo said. 'And that's why you should not run around with such heavy shopping.' She nodded at Sarah's bags. 'As a woman, I understand you. I'm also proud and want to show the world I am strong – but it's a man's job to carry things.'

'Oh, George does... did help me,' Sarah said, feeling it was unfair of Jo to think that she was entirely alone against the world in her struggle. 'So does Mark... when I can catch him and ask him to do it, that is.'

'Oh, the problems with teenage sons,' Jo said. 'I know all about it. I've raised a son and two daughters, as you know. But that's something to start with,' she added. 'Show your husband you care about him and his health. He should feel needed.'

'Yes, I could do that.' Sarah felt foolish for not thinking of it herself.

'Now I want you to lie down and rest,' Jo said. 'And later I will give you a lift home.'

'Are you sure?'

'Of course I am!' Jo exclaimed in mock indignation. 'I'm free, I don't have any classes today. I wouldn't offer if I wasn't! Oh, and another thing,' she added. 'I'd like you to make a few more dresses for me. Could we meet sometime in the near future?'

'Yes, of course! I'd love to make them for you,' Sarah replied, smiling weakly. Then she lay down on the settee in Jo's living room, grateful for her hospitality. She needed this rest — there was no chance she would get home on her own without respite. The weariness of the day and the conversation with Jo had taken their toll and she did not even notice as she dozed off.

It was late in the afternoon when Sarah woke up. As she was sitting in Jo's car on the way home, the events of the day were twisting inside her mind. Why had she fainted? She had been exhausted before — but never to the point of passing out in the middle of the city.

Her thoughts returned to her conversation with Jo. How could she save George? The more he drank, the more the distance between them seemed to increase. And she needed to speak to Mark as well. Just to make sure that he would not do anything rash or get into any trouble.

Sarah raised her eyes towards the roof of the car and folded her hands in prayer.

God, help me, please, she thought.

Chapter 5

George

George Davies was pacing the floor in the living room. He had had a short day at work and came home, hoping to find his wife and talk to her. Yet, she was not at home. Where could she be? It was unlike her to stay out for a long time.

The thoughts about the events of the day before were twisting and twirling in his mind like a swarm of moths around a light bulb. First of all, unlike the previous times when he had been drunk, he remembered the evening before in more detail than he wanted. As if watching it on TV, he repeatedly saw his hand swinging forward and hitting Sarah across the face. Remorse was gnawing at him and he was trying to form decent words of apology; pacing the floor, he was muttering under his breath:

'Sarah… I've been thinking about yesterday… No,' he said, dropping his voice. 'Sarah, I wanted to apologise for yesterday… No,' he said again, running his fingers through his hair, and sighed. Whatever he said, it sounded lame and unconvincing. He had never been a man of words, he had always been a man of deeds.

A rumbling engine interrupted his thoughts. Then car doors were opened and closed with a slap and a loud click.

'Thank you very much. It was very kind of you,' he heard Sarah's voice through the open window. He glanced outside and saw a car driving away. His wife was entering the house, her hands full of bags.

'Where have you been?' George asked. 'I was starting to worry.'

'Oh...' her voice was stiff. George felt a pang of guilt shoot through his stomach. 'It was Jo, my friend and Mark's teacher. She gave me a lift. I've been to her place.'

'What for?'

This sounded forced and more abrupt than he had intended it to be.

'She's my friend,' Sarah said, somewhat sadly. 'And I must be interested in our son's school life. I like to talk to her outside school, you know.'

George did know. Sarah attended all teacher-parent meetings for Mark – she had more time for this as she worked part-time in an office and sometimes from home when altering or even making clothes for her work colleagues – but she hated the formal setting. She did not like institutions at all (given her past, this was understandable) and preferred to meet people in their homes if possible.

'Sarah, I...' George started, feeling awkward. 'Well... I just wanted to say I'm sorry for what happened last night.' There. He had said it. 'It felt as if someone else was doing it. As if I were watching it from the outside, if you know what I mean.'

'From the outside?' Sarah repeated.

'Look... it's not the way I am,' George was no poet and hated to speak metaphorically. 'You know it's not. I am not a violent man. I... I am really, really sorry. I just don't know what got into me, really.'

'It's good to know you regret it,' Sarah said. 'Think next time.'

George felt the heavy choking feeling in his chest subside. Sarah was still mad at him, but she saw that he was sorry and now he'd try to make up for the trouble he'd caused. George's eyes moved towards the bags.

'Let me help you with those,' he said, nodding towards them. He took the bags and carried them to the kitchen after Sarah.

'I think I will have a bit more work these coming months,' Sarah said as George was unpacking the bags. 'Mrs Blake... Jo wants me to make her a few dresses for the summer.'

'That's good,' George said. He knew Sarah liked sewing and was very happy each time she got any work. 'So you will be seeing her more often, won't you?'

'I suppose so,' she said.

'George,' she added after a brief pause. 'You're a smart man – that's why I married you. I know what your workmates will say, but I also want you to listen to me. Is your health important to you?'

George wasn't surprised to hear this question. They had talked about it before. 'Of course it is,' he said. 'And I'm in good health,' he added.

'I want you to stay in good health,' she said. 'And you don't have to be a doctor to know that drinking will ruin it for you. Not to mention what happened yesterday. I want you to get a grip and stay within your limits, George. You don't want to end up like your father.'

The mention of his father made George scowl. He didn't like the fact that Sarah was bringing him into the conversation, but he couldn't say anything against it – deep down he felt that she was right.

'I will,' he said. 'I want to keep my health. You're right.'

Chapter 6

Mark

Mark was lying on his bed upstairs. He could hear the faint murmur of his parents' voices, but couldn't quite figure out what they were talking about. Well, he was glad they were not shouting. Perhaps it was a step towards making up?

'Hey, look who's outside!' he heard his father say, louder this time. Curious, Mark slid off the bed and went towards the open window. From the top floor, he could observe the back garden of their house, as well as several others, belonging to the neighbours. Neat but low hedges separated the back garden of the Davies' house and the one that belonged to Oak – an old widower with a few strange habits. Oak was a local celebrity for lack of a better word. Mad in his own, harmless way.

People said many things about Oak, starting from the fact that, of course, it wasn't his real name, but then no one knew what his name was. People said he came from Edinburgh and used to be a very intelligent and successful man. Apparently, he had two Oxford degrees – one in law and one in maths. He worked as a banker in London and was happily married. Then, one day, his wife died under mysterious circumstances. Grief drove the man to do some bizarre things: he travelled to the remotest places in Scandinavia, climbed the tallest mountains apparently in search of his wife's wandering spirit. Finally, during one of his exploits he fell off a cliff, almost to his death. Nobody knew how he ended up in Birmingham. His body was healed, but after that, he started behaving oddly.

Ever since Mark could remember, Oak had always been in a world of his own, wandering the streets, talking to himself. Another strange feature of the old man was the way he dressed. He always wore a woollen cloak and linen robes, over which he threw furs in winter. A piece of rope was his belt. With his long hair and bushy grey beard, he could easily have passed for a Celtic druid.

This time, Oak was in his garden, kindling a fire and throwing herbs into it. Mark's window was open and he could hear the man chanting to himself:

'Nature is awakening. The Earth is getting stronger, and the fire burning inside her womb pushes the grass upwards, warms the tree roots, planting blossoms onto their boughs. The Goddess is fertile. She is waiting and her waiting is not in vain. Very soon she will conceive a new life.'

The man threw a bunch of dried grass into the fire he had just lit and bowed his head.

'Goddess, please, accept these herbs, a gift taken from the Earth that will soon become Air through the cleansing power of Fire!

'The God walks across the grassy mead,' Oak continued chanting. 'His chest is broad for he is strong, and as he breathes, the living air fills his lungs and invigorates the body through the blood that sweeps through his veins like a torrent. Where the God's foot falls, a pit is left in the ground and rivers bring their water for a lake to take shape. His lips drink from the mountain spring and his body is bathed in sunlight. The God has matured and youth can be sensed in his heart and his loins. His strength needs to find an outlet, a possibility to be shown and applied. Very soon he will meet the one who will receive his strength!'

Mark wanted to turn away from the window – he had seen enough of old Oak's wizardry to write this one off as uninteresting. But something else caught his eye – his parents went outside and his father was fixing the washing line that had broken in February while his mother was pointing where she wanted it to go. It was the first time in weeks he had seen his parents doing something together.

The scene in the back garden he was witnessing sent Mark's thoughts back to Tandi. What a strange girl! He had spent the last twenty-four hours thinking about what she had said to him.

Because you'll meet me here, at this very bench this Saturday at 2 o'clock.

Should he go? Of course he should, she told him to! But it felt strange, to come to meet someone he hardly knew. It really sounded like… like an invitation to a date, although it was not like he would imagine a date to be. He just didn't know what to make of it.

Another thing he did not like was the fact that this girl was calling the shots. Her lack of understanding and tact towards his situation annoyed him. What annoyed him even more was that he had to admit she was in the right and he was in the wrong, having behaved the way he did.

But it was because of her that his anger disappeared. Before falling asleep the night before, he was sure he would oversleep school and wake up towards the last lesson, yet this morning he woke up earlier than his alarm clock rang, and could not force himself to fall back to sleep. After having tossed and turned for a few minutes, he decided it was no use and did what he always did to pass the time. One of the floorboards in his room was loose. He had a knife, a few pieces of wood and a bag for shavings hidden underneath. He took them out and started carving.

His hands did it before his mind could comprehend it: the four-legged wooden creature that emerged from under his knife clearly had the muzzle of a Labrador retriever.

Mark's thoughts returned to the present. He started thinking hard. Well, she had invited him to meet her. Whatever the reason for it, they would have to go somewhere. But where?

And suddenly he knew. The realisation was so abrupt he felt stupid for not thinking of it before. He had never told anyone... never shown anyone. He would take her to his special place.

He didn't know why he felt this way, but he was certain that he wanted to share his most treasured secret with Tandi, the girl he hardly knew.

Chapter 7

Mark

The next day, it was Saturday and Mark went to the park to meet Tandi. He had absolutely no idea what to expect. The situation of his parents occupied his mind more than this 'date' for the lack of a better word. He never told them where he was going – but then it was his business, after all.

Tandi came at two o'clock sharp, as she had promised. She brought her Labrador Spot with her, too.

'Hello,' she said. Mark returned the greeting and then gestured towards the far end of the park. The girl nodded and they started walking, Spot running around them and sniffing at Mark's jeans. All of a sudden, he started feeling nervous around her. Why was that? She certainly didn't make him feel uncomfortable. On the contrary, he found her easier to talk to than most girls at his school.

'To be honest, I doubted whether you'd come,' Tandi said.

'Why?' Mark replied. 'Did you think I would run away after all?'

'As you said – out of spite.'

'I thought you weren't taking my words seriously,' Mark said with a grin, tilting his head.

'I thought you were the master of your words,' Tandi answered in the same cheeky way. 'But you didn't run away after all.'

'Fair enough. I didn't,' Mark said. 'Instead, I decided to take you somewhere.'

Tandi laughed and said:

'And how many places did you think of?'

The list was short – there was only one place Mark wanted to show Tandi. But he said:

'Why, billions, of course! And they were all brilliant.'

'And the winner is?'

Despite his still inexplicable desire to share his secret with Tandi, Mark decided to play the secretive card for as long as he could manage.

'Follow me and find out,' he said.

'A guy with a secret and a surprise?' she said. 'Well, that's something to watch out for! Let's go then. Come on, Spot!' she called the dog, then put two fingers in her mouth and whistled loudly. A few lazy pigeons rose up in the air and landed a good dozen steps further away.

'Hey, that was nice,' Mark said, astounded.

'What was?'

'Well, your whistling. You could give any lad a head start!'

'Oh right?' Tandi said. 'It's funny, though: guys compliment girls on many things, but whistling isn't often one of them.'

Compliment?

'It's not *really* a compliment, is it?' he said.

'What's the matter?' Tandi asked. 'Are you, like, afraid to pay a compliment?'

Mark did not expect this question.

'I'm not afraid of anything of the sort,' he blurted out.

'Well, you were brave enough to accept my invitation,' Tandi said with a smile. 'That's saying something.'

Mark gave her a puzzled look.

'What do you mean? Why would I be afraid to accept it?'

'Why, you never know,' Tandi answered in a mock-conspiratorial voice. 'It's a dangerous world, it is. I may've arranged to meet you and then brought an armed gang with me!'

'Nah, you don't look like the gang type to me,' Mark said. 'If you'd wanted to harm me, you'd have followed me to my door and then sent me some notes saying, like "I know where you live" and so on.'

Tandi laughed heartily in a guttural voice and said:

'You watch way too many horror films. But where are we?' she asked, looking around. 'I don't think I've been here before.'

Mark was pleased to see that the girl did not recognise the place. He was in control of his secret.

'Exactly,' he said. 'The place I'm taking you to is off the beaten track. I wouldn't be surprised if there were, like, ten of us in the whole of Birmingham who knew what's really hidden in here. It's astonishing how many people live in the same place all their lives and see nothing but their street and the nearby alley. Some folk have lived like that for sixty-odd years.'

'It's true,' Tandi said. 'Often the strangest things happen under our very noses, without us ever realising. Really cool stuff can be hiding, you know, behind the most mundane exterior. My auntie told me there was a news report on the telly about a guy who discovered an Indian treasure in his basement while he was refurbishing it.'

'Yeah, I've heard about that one, too' Mark said, his mind wandering. He and Tandi had left the last houses behind, crossed the ancient bridge that arched over the dark water of the canal and entered the wild-looking park on the other bank. Everything was in bloom. Spring really had come early this year. As they were approaching his special place, Mark started to feel a shivery tingling in his chest. He had never acted on stage, but this was the closest he had ever come to stage fright. He got this feeling every time he picked up a piece of wood and took a knife in his hand. This was a feeling of creative anticipation. Something unseen before by others was about to be revealed.

Mark stopped, exhaled and said:

'We're almost there.'

UNDER THE DARK WATER

Tandi looked around, first at the canal that stretched to their right, then at the ivy that covered the walls of the canal and finally, at the brick wall with a rusty iron door locked with a padlock on their left. Mark looked at the puzzled expression on her face and smiled.

'What do you mean?' Tandi asked. 'We're at the canal and there's just an old factory here.'

'It's not just any old factory,' Mark said. 'Before we go any further, I need to ask you a question. Can you keep a secret?'

It was the same question his Grandpa Chris had asked him when he first showed this place to him. Mark remembered that day as if it was yesterday. He was only six years old and had just finished the first year of school. He was having breakfast with Grandpa Chris, and after they had finished their morning tea, his grandfather wiped his mouth, put the napkin down and asked:

'Mark, my boy, how old are you now?'

'Six, Grandpa Chris,' the boy said, 'and five months.'

'You're a big boy now. Now tell me, Mark, can you keep a secret?'

Mark didn't need to think too long to answer this question.

'Of course I can,' he said. 'I'm not some kind of chatterbox.'

'Of course you're not,' Grandpa Chris said, smiling. The smile always made his eyes sparkle. 'Today I want to show you something and I want this to be our secret. Do you promise me you won't tell anyone about it?'

'I do,' Mark said, now eager to know the secret. Grandpa Chris always had a way of making him very interested in everything he was about to tell or show him.

'It's outside,' he said. 'Come on, let's get dressed, and let's go!'

They walked through the familiar streets of their neighbourhood. Eventually, the densely packed houses ended, the roads became narrower and they turned onto a public footpath running through the fields where the farmers' horses were grazing.

They reached the canal and walked along it. It was still rather early and Mark felt like they were the only people awake at that hour. There was no traffic noise and not a single narrowboat in sight, only birds chirruping in the treetops.

Finally, the outline of an old building emerged from behind the trees. It looked like a derelict factory which had fallen into disrepair a long time ago. The majority of the windows on the top floor were smashed and the walls at the top were falling apart with bricks missing from them.

'We're here,' Grandpa Chris said.

'But Grandpa,' Mark said. 'It's just an old factory.'

Grandpa Chris smiled and pulled a largish jagged key out of his pocket. The same key that Mark now wore around his neck day and night.

'It's not just any old factory,' Mark repeated to Tandi, walking towards an old rusty door. 'It's *my* old factory.'

He inserted the key into the padlock and turned it. The lock clicked, Mark removed it and the door swung open. Tandi looked inside and all she could say was:

'Wooow.'

Any boy would have given the world for a secret half as fascinating as the one Mark had. Many boys would have blurted this secret out to anyone who would care to listen. Mark was not like other boys, and he kept it to himself. It was a place that he could truly call his own. It was his fortress, his treasury, and sadly, recently it had also become his refuge. He still wasn't sure why he hadn't gone there the night he met Tandi, but most of the time when his father drank and his parents quarrelled, he would go to the far end of the canal and hide inside his own abandoned factory.

Inside, everything had been made suitable for living – comfort was minimal, but it was warm and safe. Simple wooden furniture (either ancient, or second-hand, or simply assembled from pieces that someone had discarded); a makeshift brick fireplace with a tin drainpipe for a chimney; and a huge collection of strange objects that seemed valuable and worthless at the same time. Old globes, maps, pens and simple workman's tools like hammers, wooden planes, files, pliers and saws; shelves of old dusty books; boxes filled with bric-a-brac; some mysterious objects covered with heavy cloths… the large room inside the abandoned factory resembled an attic or cellar of an old house where many generations had lived, forgetting to tidy up, but the shafts of light coming through the stained windows made it look more like a laboratory of a mad scientist.

'What is this place?' Tandi asked, looking around. 'And where did all these objects come from?'

'Some of them, I brought here,' Mark replied, picking up some firewood from the corner and throwing it onto the fireplace. 'Others have been here for ages.'

'Where did you get the keys? Do you own this place?'

'My grandpa left it to me,' Mark said. He stuffed some old newspaper between the sticks and struck a match. The crumpled newspaper caught fire and soon flames were dancing on the crackling wood.

'It's a bit chilly here, you know,' Mark said. 'The sun hasn't warmed the building throughout yet.'

'My grandpa showed me everything in here,' he added. 'The books, the bric-a-brac in the chests… and after he showed it to me the first time, he gave me a key. I've had it ever since. Really, I don't even know where he got all this stuff from,' he added, looking around. 'You know, you could spend days in here looking at all of this.'

'I bet you did just that,' Tandi said.

'I did,' Mark admitted. 'It's a great place. And now you are its secret keeper.'

'How do you know I was telling the truth when I said I could keep a secret?' Tandi asked suddenly with a cheeky smile.

Mark shrugged.

'Guess I'll have to trust you on that one.'

Suddenly there was a crash as many objects fell onto the ground behind them.

'Spot, you little bugger!' Tandi said sharply. The black Labrador had pulled the edge of the cloth that covered one of the tables and everything that was under it fell on the floor with a succession of thuds.

'Spot, let go of that cloth now! He's jealous,' she explained to Mark. 'I'm talking to you and not looking at him, and he's trying to get my attention.'

But Mark did not listen. His attention was focused on the objects on the floor as the cloth covering them was being pulled away. Tandi followed Mark's gaze and her eyes widened.

'Mark, what is this?' she asked, bending down and picking up a carved wooden duck. Tandi's fingers slid along the duck's back where fine lines of ornate feathers were engraved.

'It's beautiful!' she said.

Spot had uncovered his secret. There was something within the old factory that Mark had wanted to keep hidden – at least for the time being: his collection of carved wooden figures. He had made them all with his own hands, using only his pen knife.

'Did you make them yourself?' Tandi asked.

Mark hesitated for a moment and then said:

'Yes. My grandpa taught me. To carve, and to paint them, I mean.'

There was one figure that wasn't in the room – the dog whose muzzle conspicuously resembled the Labrador retriever that was standing next to him. He had left it in his bedroom under the loose floorboard. He was relieved that he had not brought it there – that would have been embarrassing!

Tandi started picking other carved objects up and examining them.

'They're wonderful!' she said. 'You've got everything, dogs, sheep, kangaroos, even a dragon! They look great!'

'Thanks.'

'You don't sound too convinced or happy,' Tandi remarked. Mark took a deep breath and said:

'Well… It's just the conditions I made them in. I carved most of them during the past six months, when I was coming here…'

'To be on your own?' Tandi finished the sentence for him.

'To be away. Carving was my way of being free from the problems.'

Tandi raised her eyebrows at his remark but said nothing.

'You really do have talent,' she said. 'Why are you hiding them?'

'I don't like to blow my own trumpet. It's more for myself than for other people. And I don't think they're that special.'

Tandi looked at the figurines for a moment and then said:

'Teach me. I want to carve something. Is it hard?'

'Well, not really,' Mark said, taken slightly aback by this sudden request. 'All you need is a knife, a piece of wood and some patience. My grandpa said that the hardest part is to imagine the thing you're making – as if it's ready, like, polished and painted. Next, you take a piece of wood and cut off bits and shape it until you get what you'd imagined.'

'I have patience,' Tandi said. 'But I don't have a knife.'

'You can borrow mine,' Mark said, pulling his pen knife out of his pocket and extending it to her. He rummaged through the drawers of an old chest and found another one. 'I'll use this one,' he said.

'Take a small stick from the corner,' Mark instructed her. 'I'll teach you the first thing my grandpa taught me – how to make a wooden bait for fishing.'

Tandi took a stick, opened Mark's knife and sat on a chair, facing him.

'Imagine the shape of a small fish – like, three inches long,' Mark said. 'Its body gets narrower towards the tail, and the belly is a bit wider than the back. Now leave yourself plenty of stick to hold and carve at the other end, away from yourself. Actually, here,' he said, sitting opposite her. 'Copy me. Repeat what I do. Gently, shave off thin layers, don't cut too deep.'

Mark felt very strange when explaining this. He had never been a teacher, let alone taught a girl something. It felt awkward and unfamiliar, but he had to admit he liked doing it. After about half an hour, Mark was polishing both round-bellied fish figurines and carving scales into their sides. Tandi was watching him curiously, which made Mark feel even more awkward but pleased.

'Now we need to attach some hooks,' Mark said, inserting his fish into a vice. He took two triple fishing hooks from a box on one of the shelves and found a couple of stainless steel pins with large heads. He attached the hooks to the pins and carefully hammered the pins into the wooden fish's belly. He did the same with the other fish and attached a ball of lead to the front of each figurine.

'Now we can paint them to look like real fish,' he said, opening the cupboard and taking out several tubes and cans of acrylic paint. Spot, who had until then been lying on the floor and watching them calmly, raised his head and sniffed the air curiously.

'What haven't you got in here!' Tandi exclaimed.

'This place is meant to be a workshop,' Mark said, opening a can of paint. 'My grandfather used to work in here. He made furniture.'

'That's a nice job,' Tandi said. 'Do you have any made by him?'

'Half of the stuff in our house was made by him,' Mark said. He had finished applying the silvery-bluish paint onto the wood and was now sitting by the fire, turning the wooden fish in his hands for the paint to dry quicker. 'In my room it's the bed and the wardrobe he's made.'

'Wicked!' Tandi said. 'I'd love to have furniture made by someone I know. Mine's all from the factory.'

'Yeah, he was a great carpenter,' Mark said. 'Wish I could be like that. I can only make a shelf and carve, like, a wooden sheep to put on it.'

'Never too late to learn,' Tandi said.

The paint on the fish figurines had dried. Mark put them on the table and opened several more tubes of paint.

'Wanna decorate your fish?' he asked, offering Tandi a brush.

'Yeah,' she said, picking through the tubes of paint. 'We could draw, like, an outline of the scales with dark grey.'

'Only on one of them,' Mark said. 'On the other one, I wanna have something like small specks of yellow and red. Should look attractive for the monster pikes.'

'Monster pikes?' Tandi said, laughing. 'Where do you want to catch them, in the canal?'

'Well,' Mark said, 'in some parts of the canal the water is so murky it can easily hide something like a giant squid!'

'You *do* watch too many horror films, I told you,' Tandi said, confidently outlining the scales on her bait. Mark watched her hands move.

'You're pretty good with a brush,' he said. 'Do you also have a talent I don't know about?'

'You're quite observant for a guy,' Tandi said, but she seemed somewhat wary of the fact that Mark had noticed it. 'Yes, I like drawing and painting, but I don't show my work to people. I don't think it's that good.'

'Maybe you should show it to someone,' Mark said. 'I still think my carvings are nothing special, but you seem to like them.'

'It's not the same,' Tandi said. 'Yours really are good.'

But Mark was not going to give up that easily. Unexpectedly, curiosity got the better of him. After all, Tandi now knew two of his secrets. He felt that he had the right to know something more about her. Somehow he knew what he needed to say.

'I thought you were brave,' he said, casually.

'Excuse me?'

'I thought you were brave,' he repeated.

'I am!' she said, hotly. 'Show me a tree, I'll climb it and jump down if you want!'

'I'm not asking you to climb any trees,' Mark said. 'I'm asking you to show your drawings to someone. Me, for example.'

'You? Why you of all people?'

'Because, of all people, I'm the most curious one,' Mark said in the same casual tone.

'Well, alright then,' Tandi burst out. 'But just to shut you up so you never say I'm not brave again.'

'Deal,' Mark said. 'When? Next Saturday?' The words left his mouth before he could think about them. He hoped he hadn't sounded too hopeful or desperate.

'I'm busy next week,' Tandi said. He was surprised – she sounded almost apologetic. 'Saturday two weeks from now?'

'Alright,' he said, trying to sound casual. 'Just don't chicken out.'

'I'm no chicken,' Tandi retorted. 'But you… you're, like, such a cocky cock-a-doodle-doodling rooster!'

Chapter 8

Sarah

Sarah turned on the taps and watched as foam formed on the surface of steaming hot water in the bathtub. George was at work and Mark was at school, so it was the perfect time to take some care of herself and think some things over. She looked into the mirror above the sink, examining her naked body. For a thirty-eight-year-old woman, she looked quite decent. Maybe tonight she should surprise George? Put on some nice underwear, you know… If he comes home sober, that is. She'd only slept with a drunken man twice in her life (that was long before she met George), and both times the experience had been horrible. Sarah shook her head to make the memories go away.

She stepped into the hot water and lay inside the spacious bathtub, listening to the whirring of the steam extractor fan and the silent rustling as the foam bubbles popped, breathing in the aroma of honeysuckle and milk. The water surrounded her, and she felt her tense muscles relaxing, but her mind was all over the place. She needed to think some things over and she knew only one way to do it.

'Hi again, Mary Beth,' Sarah said quietly.

'Hello,' the crystal-clear voice said. 'Glad you came. I thought you'd forgotten me now that you've got Jo.'

'Oh, come on, don't be like that!' Sarah said. She knew that Mary Beth was probably just being silly, but for an imaginary friend, she had quite a difficult personality. 'You know perfectly well I can't tell her half of the things I can tell you. You'll always be my most special friend.'

Sarah could feel Mary Beth smile. A bit of flattery never failed to work. Besides, this was true. Sarah had found it hard to bond with adults in her life. She had been born out of wedlock and had grown up at the Josiah Mason orphanage in Birmingham in the 1950s after her mother, an ironmonger's daughter, died in childbirth and her father, whom she never knew, emigrated to the United States shortly after getting her mother pregnant. Some time later, he sent a letter to the orphanage saying he would come back for his daughter, but he never did, so the girl was passed around between the orphanage and foster families.

'So, what is it this time?' Mary Beth asked.

'It's George. And Mark. My family. I...' Sarah stopped as something stuck in her throat, making her voice break. 'I'm scared. I'm really scared, more than I've ever been in my life!'

After she uttered these words, tears started flowing down her face uncontrollably and she lay there in the bathtub, sobbing, her palms clutching at her shoulders. Fear paralysed her and she couldn't think straight anymore. Still, she felt strangely relieved after admitting this to Mary Beth. Even with Jo, she could not open up as much as with the imaginary friend she'd had for the most of her life.

'You shouldn't be,' Mary Beth said. *'Trust in the Lord with all your heart and do not lean on your own understanding.* Isn't that what the nuns told you at the orphanage?'

'Yes, but it's not easy to keep hoping and believing when everything you've been building for such a long time keeps crumbling down!' Sarah whispered, tears still rolling from her eyes.

Mary Beth nodded understandingly.

'I agree,' she said. 'Despite the religious education we've both received, applying what you've learnt is not easy. The nuns at the orphanage gave us all a lot of good advice. Not everyone listened to it, though.'

That was true. Sarah's thoughts returned to her childhood. The austere, ascetic environment of the orphanage run by Anglican nuns was her first home. She grew up surrounded by strictness, with the many rules of the Church on one side and the hardships of post-war Britain on the other. She remembered food rationing, and one of her earliest happy memories was the day when it ended.

She often recalled how the nuns in the orphanage told them every day, 'God gave you life. Do something good with it!' Some heeded this advice and some did not. Sarah considered herself one of those who did. Growing up, she saw a lot of things going wrong: rebellious teenage girls running away from the orphanage building and plunging into the dizziness of the swinging sixties; she saw them coming back, secretly vomiting in the bathroom in the evening because they were drunk or early in the morning because they were pregnant. She saw some younger, cuter girls being adopted and moving to their new families. This happened to Mary Elizabeth, or Mary Beth as everyone called her, a very kind and helpful girl with a beautiful smile – the only girl she counted as a friend. She had never heard from her since she was adopted. She had no real friends in the orphanage; there was just a sense of some stern shared purpose, and rules, and austerity.

All of this made Sarah close up and become withdrawn. Her marks suffered and she became more reserved, especially after Mary Beth was gone. This was when another, imaginary Mary Beth appeared in her life, and never left her side since.

'You have always told me everything about George and Mark, Sarah,' Mary Beth said. 'I know what they both mean to you.'

'They're all I have,' Sarah whispered. 'All I have, Mary Beth. My only family. I can't afford to lose them.'

'You will not lose them,' Mary Beth said firmly. George is doing better now, you know that. And I think you've got a role to play in this. Admit it: he's been making more effort for you, for the family. He's been more active in bed, too. Maybe he's trying to show that drinking has not affected his manhood.'

Sarah blushed.

'Mary Beth, you can't talk like this! Not even I talk that way.'

But Sarah knew that her forthright imaginary friend had a point. George had recently been a better husband in more ways than one. Still, she felt anxious.

'I may have won the battle,' she said. 'But I'm not so sure about the war.'

'Oh, come on! Don't lose confidence now! And have faith.' Now Sarah could also hear anxiety in Mary Beth's crystal-clear voice.

'It's not easy to have confidence or faith,' she said. She was not sure where this conversation was going. The fear had let go of her, but there was nothing to replace it. She felt empty.

'What do you know about faith?' Mary Beth asked suddenly.

The question took Sarah aback.

'Are you asking me seriously?' she said. Mary Beth nodded. 'Well, faith means many things. For example, I've been raised in the Christian faith and that's a part of me. I've also been told to have faith in God and in myself. But it's not always been easy as we both know.'

'That's not all,' Mary Beth replied. 'You speak about your faith as if it were a habit – something you do because you've been doing it for long enough. I remember what you were like as a young girl. You would go to mass and pray and all that. Why did you do it? Why do you still do it? Just out of habit? Or because you were told to?

'I'd say your faith has been a choice. At least from a certain point. It became more than a habit. Neither you nor George had it easy in life and both of you had a difficult relationship with religion. George's stepfather could not repair the damage that his father had done. You saw a lot of things happen that should not have happened in a place run by priests and nuns. You closed up and living with a vicar's family couldn't open you up to people or your faith. And yet, your faith is much stronger now than it was when everything that reminded you of faith surrounded you. After all, where did you go after your first date with George?'

'I went to church,' Sarah said. 'I was… so confused.'

'Who wouldn't be? But it was a choice, not force of habit. And talking of opening up – it was thanks to George that you started trusting yourself, and other people, wasn't it?'

'Yes, it was,' Sarah admitted. 'That's true.'

'You see, faith means not only believing in God,' Mary Beth said, sitting on the edge of the bathtub and kicking the thick foam with her tiny legs. 'It also means being faithful to the brightest, most precious memories of your life. It means declaring your loyalty to the time when you've made the greatest discovery in your life – that there is a person about whom you care more than about yourself. Someone you can trust with your most guarded secrets. For you, this someone was George and no one else.'

'Yes,' Sarah said. 'George and no one else.'

Her thoughts raced back to the times at the orphanage. When the imaginary Mary Beth replaced the real one, Sarah became more withdrawn and reclusive. She took part in everyday activities, but no more than necessary. Between the ages of eleven and fourteen she rarely gossiped and never shared a single secret with anyone. When she was fourteen, the orphanage closed and Sarah was transferred to a normal school. After leaving the orphanage, she was taken in by foster family in Worcester. It was the family of a middle-aged vicar called Father Grahame Clifton. The other family members were the vicar's wife who was the family's order-keeper and his sister – a singleton who liked a glass of sherry and a good laugh. She stayed with them until she turned eighteen. The vicar's family were kind people, but somehow she never developed a close relationship with them. Perhaps it was the fact that she was closed up – she didn't know. Sarah didn't like overanalysing herself. Still, the Clifton family sent her cards for Christmas and Easter after she got a job and moved into a council flat in Birmingham, and she sent them cards too, even now. She had also stayed in touch with the two nuns who were in charge of educating the group of girls she belonged to – Sister Grey and Sister Margaret. After the orphanage closed, they moved to the Holy Cross Convent in Leicestershire. She had been able to visit them once or twice since then, but coming to the convent always felt very strange. Despite feeling quite comfortable in church, she felt somehow alien in the austere environment of the monastery.

Still, despite all the care that the foster family gave her, it could not take away the unwillingness to open up that she'd developed in her early years. She did not open up to anyone and had no real family until she met George.

The first encounter couldn't have been more prosaic – she dropped her purse while she was out shopping at Woolworth's and before she realised it, there he was, a young man in a chequered worker's shirt, his ruffled hair giving him an attractively rugged look. He picked up her purse and handed it to her.

'Hi,' he said. 'I think you've dropped this.' Then he smiled at her and added: 'I'm George.'

Sarah blushed and introduced herself.

'Thank you,' she said, taking the purse from his hand and suddenly feeling very awkward. 'I didn't even notice, that would've been quite a loss. It's my payday today, you know…' Her voice trailed off. What was she doing? Telling an absolute stranger the story of her life! That was certainly not acceptable.

'Really? Where do you work?' George asked. She was so grateful for the fact that he did not notice her embarrassment that she didn't even realise the second question was also a personal one.

'I'm a shop assistant,' she said, casually. 'A simple worker, like anyone else.'

'A simple worker like anyone else?' George repeated. 'Does that mean you'd like to be a special worker, doing something else?' he asked with a smile. That simple, kind smile in his face, red from working all day in the sun… Sarah responded before she could stop herself.

'I… I'd like to be a dressmaker,' she said, feeling more and more embarrassed. 'To make nice evening dresses for ladies, you know.'

'Sounds good,' George said. 'Have you started learning?'

'Learning what?'

'Well, the craft. I don't know all the ins and outs, but there's all that cutting and stitching and adjusting... Do you know how to? I'm a builder, you know. Never needed to wear anything tailor-made.'

'Oh, I can sew,' Sarah said. 'I grew up surrounded by nuns who taught us how to do all the household jobs.'

Really, what am I doing? Sarah thought. *Why am I telling him all these things?* But she couldn't help trusting this man and they kept talking until they left the shop, and on the way home, George invited her out the following week. She blushed and agreed.

'You certainly did blush a lot that day and some other days after that, too!' Mary Beth said, pulling her back into reality. 'You were like a ripe tomato, love.'

'Mary Beth, what's the matter? You're talking like Jo now!'

Mary Beth chuckled, obviously pleased with herself.

'You liked him right from the start, admit it!'

'I did,' Sarah said. 'It was something... It was everything about him, down to his job.'

'Yes, you even liked the fact that he was a builder. There was something so masculine in his weathered face, the muscles on his arms and chest and the fact that he could do all the DIY by himself. But the arms and the chest mattered more…' Mary Beth said in a dreamy voice.

'Stop praising him!' Sarah said and threw a handful of foam at her. 'I'm starting to feel jealous! Have you been looking at him too much? Because you're noticing way more than you should!'

'Oh, don't be jealous,' Mary Beth cried in a mock pleading tone. 'I wouldn't have noticed any of this if you hadn't told me about it yourself!'

This was true as well. Sarah told her friend everything. How her hands trembled uncontrollably as she was getting ready for the first date with George. And how her knees shook when George rang the doorbell of his parents' house and then took her hand reassuringly as they came to meet them for the first time. How their son was born – a spitting image of his father. George had been with her throughout the pregnancy and all the sleepless nights. They shared everything. She had always felt his support. Tears welled up in her eyes at the thought of losing that support. It was as if something was yanking her hand out of George's grip and replacing her husband's firm, callused hand with a cold, slimy tentacle.

'How dear are George and Mark to you?' A challenge rang in Mary Beth's crystal voice.

'What is this stupid question? More than anything else in my life!'

'Then you should decide what is stronger – your fear or your desire to protect them.'

Mary Beth was right. There was no point in being afraid. George and Mark were her only family. They were all she had, and she would not give them up under any circumstances. Come what may, she was going to fight with all her strength to keep her family together. Yes, she was going to fight.

Chapter 9

George

George couldn't sleep. The sheets felt uncomfortable and sticky despite the sudden coolness of the night that had come after an incredibly hot fortnight in April. He listened to his wife's breathing in the dark; it was quiet and well-paced, but something in it gave away the tiredness that sleep could not remove. Trying not to wake her up, George swung his legs to the side of the bed, stood up and went to the bathroom.

He did his business with the lights off, flushed the toilet and went to the sink to wash his hands and face. Scattered moonlight penetrated the frosted glass of the window, and no light was needed. George looked up into the mirror and froze.

Water was dripping from the face that was looking at him – but the face was not his own. Standing in the mirror before him on its hind legs, staring at him with its oily eyes, black like the night outside the window, was a white horse.

'What the…' George murmured, before he rubbed his eyes and looked up again.

The horse took its head between its hooves and… removed it.

It was a mask. The face of a young man emerged from under it; the creature's glossy hide became loose and creased, and turned into white overalls, like the ones workers usually wear.

Every drop of water that fell back into the sink from George's face and shivering hands sounded like an explosion to him. The man in the mirror looked a bit like his own son, Mark.

'Evening, George,' he said. The smile on his lips made George cringe and shudder; yet it attracted him. *Like flowing water,* George thought, not really knowing why this particular image came to his mind. He stared at the mirror wide-eyed.

'Scared?' the figure asked. 'You shouldn't be. Yes, I am real, you're not going mad,' he added, responding to George's silence. 'I'm just as real as the fact that you're having trouble falling asleep. You've been at work all week. Aren't you wondering why you can't sleep on a Saturday night?'

Despite his astonishment, George paused at the man's words. He was a healthy man as far as he was concerned. Anyone who thought otherwise could try saying it to his face. So why would he have sleeping problems? He was tired, too – the kind of tiredness a man can experience after spending time with a woman. Sarah had been particularly kind to him the day before and today. He should have had no trouble falling asleep.

'Who are you?' he asked, finally, feeling foolish for talking to the mirror. The man behind the glass that glinted in scattered moonlight rays seemed surprised by his question.

'*Who am I?* When was the last time you looked in this mirror? Take a closer look, you might recognise me.'

George leant towards the glass and peered into the dimly-lit face. A sudden urge to pull away and switch on the light flushed over him like a breeze, but another part of him, something hidden deep inside the crevices of his mind, refused to obey that urge.

Then it dawned on him. He suppressed a gasp. The figure in the mirror nodded and spoke again.

'Yes, this is how you used to look, George. A bit like how your son looks now – am I right? Only ten years ago.' Another chilling smile appeared on the man's face and faded away. 'I see disbelief in your eyes,' he continued. 'I see you want to run your fingers down your face. You're thirty-eight, George, and grey hair is appearing at your temples and advancing upwards. You can feel your age in your bones and muscles. Thirty-eight should be like *childhood* for a man. But you... you are under constant strain and your age is showing. Your infirmity is showing.'

'Bullshit!' George mouthed. The man staring back at him remained silent as if inviting – or daring – him to say more.

'Of course I'm under strain!' George whispered with anger, leaning forward. The man in the mirror also leant towards him, and their foreheads almost touched. 'Do you realise what I'm going through?'

'As a matter of fact, I do. Grief, that's what. You are grieving, George. It's not easy to watch your sister's life ebb away and feel helpless, unable to do anything, standing just a couple of yards away from her. Or holding her hand as the ambulance is late.'

George felt a surge of cold air rush past him; it made his hair stand on end. The stranger in the mirror stared at him, unblinkingly. In the dimly-lit bathroom, the oily blotches he had for eyes looked like dark whirlpools. So mysterious. So attractive.

'How do you…?'

'Know?' the man finished for him. 'I know many things, George. I know that you are beginning to feel sick even of the job you're doing. This is what you like most – building, painting, decorating. And now you feel trapped. Or will you say that I'm making it up?'

George listened silently to the words of the stranger in the mirror. There was some truth in them – after Celia, his sister, died literally in his arms, nothing he did could satisfy him anymore. He had been brought up with a simple masculine mindset: overcome all obstacles, carry on no matter what, toughen up and be strong. His stepfather had been the most supportive and encouraging person he had ever known. Yet, luckily (or maybe unluckily) for him, all obstacles until that day had been surmountable, all unpleasant business could be sorted out, all issues fixed. He felt he was in control of his life. He had a family, a house, and a job. He used to have a drinking problem many years ago, but had also been able to overcome it. He had enough of a backbone to manage on his own.

Until the day when something that he could not control happened.

Yes, he did feel trapped. Who would blame him for that?

'Everyone has their own way of escaping the worries of this world,' the figure in the mirror continued. 'Some use drugs. Some buy whores. You have chosen a circle of friends from work – after all, they form a large part of your life, don't they, George? Spending time with your mates involves drinking. It does not prevent you from doing the work you're supposed to do, right? You could do much worse than having a pint or two with your friends.'

George remained silent. He knew where the stranger's thoughts were leading and he was not sure he wanted to follow, but kept listening.

'It is an important part of your life, George. The pub experience is not the drinking – it's the fellowship of men that brings them closer and takes away the strain. Your words, not mine, George. Do you recognise your own words?'

'Yes I do,' George snapped back. 'But I also remember what Sarah said – this is something a young, unmarried man would think. It's not the way to see the world when you've got a teenage son.'

'So, is your wife implying that she cares about your son more than you do?'

'She's not implying anything!'

'Of course she isn't,' the man in the mirror said. 'I won't even bother to say she is – I want you to see it for yourself!'

The man slipped the mask back on. There was a horse in the mirror again.

'Tell me, George,' the horse said. 'Has your wife been good to you?'

'Fuck off! That's not something I'm going to discuss. It's ridiculous, I'm talking to the mirror!'

'Of course she has. Because you have abstained from drinking. You're not going out with your mates. She doesn't understand that you need this.'

George looked up, ready to make a snide remark at the man, but words failed him. Suddenly, the face of the creature in the mirror started changing. Ripples moved all over its skin as if it were liquid. Then its features started shifting, its face began changing shape until it turned into a blur and vanished completely and George abruptly let go of the edges of the washbasin he was clutching and turned away from the mirror. That was enough. What was he doing? Talking to his own reflection? That fit nowhere with the definition of a healthy man. Cautiously, he looked over his shoulder into the dark glassy surface that reflected nothing but the darkness of the bathroom – the moon was gone, and so was the stranger in the mirror. Another thin stream of cold air came at him from the window.

George felt the tiredness of the week hit him. It felt like running into a ten-foot wall of some viscous liquid. Then the wall broke over him and all George could do was stumble towards the bed. All his muscles were aching; his ears were buzzing with fatigue and he couldn't catch any sounds outside of his own head.

'Bullshit,' he whispered. 'This must be a dream. Only a stupid dream.'

And yet, as he was shutting the bathroom door, he heard a voice coming from the corner where the mirror hung. The voice said:

'This isn't over. We'll talk again.'

Chapter 10

George

George was lying in bed next to Sarah. It was early Sunday morning and both of them could have a bit of a lie-in. Maybe later Sarah would go to church. George could not be bothered. It was not that he wasn't a religious man. He did believe in God and fitted the basic description of a Christian: someone who looks at Jesus through the eyes of his disciples. His view of the Son of God was not a philosophical one that claimed that 'yes, something does exist out there' and not a cynical one that viewed Jesus as a very good illusionist. Yet, his relationship with religion and God in particular was a rather lukewarm one. Sometimes he was even jealous of Sarah's active worship and participation in the life of the church. Christmas and Easter were almost the only times he obeyed his wife's wishes and joined his family for the services.

It had been like this for a very long time. His stepfather's death did not improve things one bit. Actually, he had hoped it would. You know, all those thoughts about the meaning of life and how fragile life is… but he did not feel anything. Nothing but a terrible emptiness. He did not want to go back to that day and chided himself for doing so, even if it was only a passing thought.

He missed his stepfather, Chris McRae, the man his mother married after separating from his real father – an angry, abusive, violent drunk. George shook his head, trying to make the troubling thoughts go away.

Sarah stretched next to him and pressed her body against his, half-asleep. George put his arm around her shoulders, placed his hand on her breast absent-mindedly and stared at the ceiling, frowning.

Sarah woke up at the touch and giggled.

'Don't tickle me,' she said.

'Why not? You're mine to tickle,' George said, hugging his wife tightly. His mind was beginning to race all over the place again, but the feeling of Sarah's touch slowed his thoughts a little, bringing him a feeling of inner peace. There she was, warm and real. It was she who had pulled him out of the dark place he had been in after his stepfather's death.

'Oh, don't be like that!' Sarah said with a smile, pressing her cheek against his chest. Suddenly George felt he needed to get up to go to the bathroom – not very romantic, but, well, he had never been a romantic person. Sometimes he wished he could write a poem for Sarah, but fixing taps and hanging shelves was also an expression of love. It was his own way of saying he cared.

The thought about the bathroom triggered the memories of the night before. He still could not believe it. It must have been a stupid dream! Even dreaming of this was implausible. A man with a horse's mask in the mirror? Talking to him? He scowled at the thought. All of this seemed too unnatural and stupid. It had been a dream. Just a stupid bloody dream.

'What's the matter?' Sarah asked. 'Why the sour face?'

George didn't know what to answer to this question. He couldn't possibly tell her the truth. How would that sound? *Hey, Sarah, you know, I was talking to the mirror yesterday. The man in it had a horse's head and he looked a bit like me when I was younger.* No, talking about it was out of the question. Dreams, or whatever, were not real. Sarah at his side was real, though. This was where his focus should be.

'It's the old stuff,' he said. 'You know, Celia and all that. My father, too.'

Sarah frowned.

'I shouldn't have reminded you of your father the other day. I know that these aren't memories you want to relive. I'm sorry.'

'No, no, it's... it's not you. It's none of your fault.'

He felt bad about lying to Sarah. And yet, he felt he simply had to keep it to himself – at least for now. The best way to deal with what he didn't understand was to ignore it. This method had worked so far, so it should work in future, he thought.

Sarah sat up in bed and slipped off her nightie.

'I still want to make up for it,' she said, pressing her body close to his under the covers. George embraced her, and the past dissolved in the present like a floe dissolves in a river in spring. The horse-man in the mirror disappeared.

There was Sarah. And there was he. And just enough time to make love.

Chapter 11

Mark

'So, here we are,' Tandi said as the bus rolled gently to the stop on Cole Bank Road. 'Come on, Spot!' she called. The black Labrador retriever stood up and Mark and Tandi got off the bus, Spot following closely at Tandi's heels.

'Been here before?' Tandi asked.

'No, actually, I haven't,' he said.

'It's one-all then. Last time you showed me something I hadn't seen before. Today it's my turn.'

'Yep, one-all,' Mark admitted. It felt strange: he considered himself to be quite an eager explorer of the city of Birmingham and prided himself on being the first one to discover a lot of things about the city that usually remained hidden to others. He should have been feeling very cheesed off now because this girl had beaten him to it! Yet, he was quite enjoying the feeling of exploring with someone else as his guide. Especially with this girl, he said to himself, grateful that people could not read his thoughts.

It had been exactly two weeks since Mark had shown Tandi his hiding place – the abandoned factory.

The weather had been great and the nature in Birmingham had changed beyond recognition: full-grown leaves in all shades of green, from lettuce to emerald, replaced the pale-green shoots that were shyly poking out of tree branches and bushes.

'What's this place called?' Mark asked when they approached a wooden fence behind which an old-looking red brick building stood, surrounded by greenery. Tandi opened the gate in the fence and they stepped into the cobbled yard. Wooden wheels that probably used to belong to old carts stood propped against the walls; next to them stood large circles made of stone.

'Are these millstones?' he asked.

Tandi nodded.

'This place is called Sarehole Mill,' she said. 'It's one of the oldest in the Midlands – like, 300 years old or something. Have you read *The Lord of the Rings*?'

'Sort of,' Mark said.

'What do you mean – sort of?'

'Well, I didn't, like, read all three books cover to cover. But I read enough to know what it's about. Why do you ask?'

'Did you know that John Tolkien, the bloke who wrote the books, grew up here, in Birmingham?'

'No, I didn't know that,' Mark said. It came as quite a surprise.

'He liked playing around here when he was little,' Tandi said. 'The green space is called the Shire Country Park.'

'No way! The Shire? That's wicked!'

'It is,' Tandi agreed. They passed an old bakehouse on their right with whitewashed walls and an enormous wood-fuelled oven inside and turned left, towards the entrance. A man wearing a blue shirt with *Birmingham City Council* embroidered on it smiled at them and said:

'Good morning to you, Sir, Madam and Dog. Enjoy your visit. This way please – but you'll need to leave the dog right here,' he added, gesturing towards the wall.

Tandi tied Spot's leash to an iron ring in the wall and started climbing a set of steep wooden stairs, and Mark followed her. The stairs led them into a room where a dark mill wheel nestled inside a large niche in the floor. The wheel was connected to a set of dented gears that were joined to a heavy millstone about a yard in diameter. There was another man in a blue shirt explaining to an elderly couple how the mill used to be operated.

'So,' the man said, pointing at the millstone. 'This stone here – the one with a hole – was fixed on top of another one, without a hole. Grains would be poured into the hole and as the water turned this large wheel over there, the gears would spin and turn the bottom stone – the one with the spindle wedged inside it, grinding the grains into fine flour. Let me show you how it worked.'

The man stepped through a tiny gate in the railings surrounding the wheel and lifted a wooden lever. The sluice gates opened and the water rushed into the opening, making the giant wheel spin.

'The wheel kept on turning all day,' the man continued, 'and corn and wheat were ground continuously. Can you imagine the amount of flour dust in the air? For this reason, it was strictly forbidden to smoke or light fires anywhere inside the mill. Flour particles are extremely flammable!'

'And about the books –' Tandi added, looking at the spinning wheel, 'I've read *The Hobbit* and *The Lord of the Rings*, cover to cover, twice.'

'Twice?' Mark said, putting the most incredulous expression he could onto his face. 'How long did that take you?'

'Time well spent, I think.'

'Come on, I mean, the books are great, but the guy can be so boring sometimes. Why would you write ten pages about how green the forest was or how brown the cliffs of Mordor were? I get the idea after two sentences, just get on with it!'

'Mark, you're so impatient,' Tandi said, laughing. 'You boys always want to get to the action and skip everything that happens between one battle and another.'

'That's not called impatience, that's just, like, common sense,' Mark answered with a nonchalant smile, walking through the spacious attic of the Mill. It reminded him somewhat of the attic in his grandfather's house, but that one was much more cluttered and full of mysterious objects. It was one of his favourite places – after the abandoned factory by the canal, of course. He could have spent hours on end there.

'You're not a big fan of literature, then?' Tandi asked.

'No, I prefer sciences,' Mark said. 'Especially chemistry and biology.'

'Let me guess,' Tandi said. 'You like chemistry because you get to blow stuff up.'

'Why, that's not true!' Mark exclaimed, pretending to be offended. 'Otherwise I would have explosives everywhere in that factory of mine. And I don't have them everywhere. I have them in a special box, hidden away from prying eyes!'

Since Tandi looked so proud of having read the books twice, suddenly Mark felt the need to boast about something as well.

'But even if I'm not a big fan of literature, I know some things about the *Lord of the Rings* books that very few people actually know,' he said.

'Really? Like what?'

'Like, can you tell me the exact date when the One Ring was destroyed?'

'Is it in the book?' Tandi asked. 'I don't remember, to be honest.'

Inside his mind, Mark pounded the air with his fist triumphantly.

'It was the twenty-fifth of March.'

'And here you are, telling me you haven't read the book thoroughly,' Tandi said, scrutinising him with her eyes.

'I haven't, honest.' Mark held up his hands in a defensive move. 'My Grandpa read them to me when I was little. He also explained why it was that day and not any other. Wanna know?'

'Yeah. Why?'

'Tolkien was a very religious man. The twenty-fifth of March is nine months before Christmas, so it's the day Mary found out she would give birth to Jesus. It was a very important day for him. In the past, it was also the day of Easter. It didn't move between March and April like it does now.'

'Wow. I didn't know that. Was your grandpa religious, too?' Tandi asked.

'He was,' Mark said after a pause. 'It's a shame I didn't get to spend a lot of time with him. He died when I was nine.'

He didn't like going back to that day. The day he lost Grandpa Chris. It was he, Mark, who discovered him lying in the guest bed in their house. He remembered that it was a very dark time for his father, too. George Davies spent most of the next three days before the funeral at Grandpa Chris's side: in the funeral home and in church with very little sleep. He slept a lot after the funeral and then spent the next two days at the cemetery, only coming home to have dinner and sleep. Eventually, he started living normally, mostly thanks to his mother's care.

Mark did not take it too well himself, either. At first, he simply blocked out all thoughts about it, pretending it had never happened. Then, slowly, he allowed faint memories of Grandpa Chris to enter his mind. After a couple of months, he turned to brighter memories until, after a long twelve months, he felt was brave enough to think about *that day*.

'He was very intelligent, too,' Mark added. 'He liked reading a lot and had a huge library. He made all the bookcases by himself, of course. Actually, I think he imagined himself to be a bit like a hobbit, you know. He liked wearing waistcoats, loved mushrooms and was very fond of plants. He had, like, a little vegetable patch in his back garden and an allotment, too.'

As he was telling all of this to Tandi, Mark felt a bit surprised: he'd never shared any information about his grandfather with anyone before. Some conversations he had with him remained secret even now because they were meant for his ears only and he wanted to keep it this way. He wanted to keep some memories only to himself – this way, they were more special. And yet, here he was, telling this girl about his life and not restraining his tongue for a second. Well, that was another first.

'Like my grandparents,' Tandi said. 'They were very religious too. I don't remember them, they died back in Jamaica before I was born, but everyone tells me about them. My grandpa had a stroke and was lying in bed for a year and a half, unable to move. My grandma took care of him all that time. People even said to her when my grandpa passed away, "You've always looked after him in such a Christian way," and she'd reply, "Is there any other way?"'

'I'm sorry to hear about your grandparents,' Mark said, feeling awkward. He felt he was terrible at conversation when it came to topics like death. Nothing he could say seemed good enough.

'And I'm sorry to hear about your grandpa,' Tandi said. Mark looked at her; she didn't seem to find this conversation awkward. Perhaps it was okay. 'You two must have been very close.'

'Yes,' Mark said, 'we were. It's really amazing how much he taught me. And my dad – he's taught me what my grandpa taught him.'

They finished exploring the mill and went out through the gates, into a sunlit meadow.

'There's another place I'd like to show you,' Tandi said, untying Spot's leash from the ring in the wall. 'It's very close, just across the road. I've kept my promise,' she added after a brief pause. 'I've brought some of my paintings.' She patted her bag. 'I can show them to you when we get there.'

'Oh, great,' Mark said, smiling. 'So you didn't chicken out after all.'

'I don't do "chickening out", Mark,' she said with mock indignation. 'Just like you didn't run away from home after I told you to meet me.'

'Fair point,' Mark said. They crossed the meadow, then crossed Wake Green Road, and walked past a dozen low-rise yellow-brick houses. Finally, they climbed over a low wall made of earth and stepped into a vast green space.

'This place is called Moseley Bog,' Tandi said. 'There used to be a pond here that supplied water to the mill. Now it's been kind of drained and turned into a park. Take care, though – the ground isn't dry everywhere. You need to walk on these,' she said, pointing at the raised boards that formed narrow winding paths among the trees.

'This place is incredible,' Mark said, looking around. He picked up a strangely-shaped branch from the ground – that could be carved into something nice later, he thought.

They walked along the path of raised boards skirting a small stream that ran through the Bog. Spot didn't care too much where he stepped, so his paws got mucky very fast. Mark felt as if they were somewhere deep in the countryside: he never knew there was a place in the middle of Birmingham where all the noises of the city could be shut out and only birdsong and the sound of the wind rustling the leaves would fill the air.

'Let's go over there,' Tandi said, pointing towards a steep hill across the brook. Mark hopped over the water and extended his hand to Tandi to help her get across. His own gesture surprised him. As soon as he did it, he thought of how stupid it looked. He knew Tandi well enough to know that she could hop over the brook by herself.

He was expecting her to ask him something like: 'Do you think I can't do it?' He was surprised again:

Tandi took his hand without a word. For a brief moment, as he held her hand in his palm, it felt... damn it, he couldn't find the words to describe it. But it definitely felt good. He tried to suppress his jaw-splitting grin.

They climbed the hill and went into a clearing.

'Here,' Tandi said, pointing towards a large log on the ground. 'We can sit here and you can see my paintings, since you want to so much.'

'All right,' Mark agreed.

'But I'm warning you – they're nothing special. I've just brought them so you can't say I'm not brave enough to show them to you.'

'Deal,' Mark said. Tandi opened her backpack and took out a large padded envelope.

'Here,' she said, extending it towards Mark. He took the envelope and opened it. There were half a dozen paintings inside – three watercolours and three done in acrylic paint on plywood.

Mark looked at them one by one. The watercolours depicted nature: a stormy sea with foam on top of the waves looking like white sheep in a field of blue swaying grass; a beach full of turtles climbing out of the sea; a forest with the sun setting behind the trees. The acrylic paintings all depicted scenes from *The Lord of the Rings* books: Gandalf and Frodo walking towards Bag-End; the eagles flying over Mount Doom; an army of Ents, legendary walking trees, marching towards the fortress of Isengard.

'They're… just incredible,' Mark said. Tandi smiled, lowering her eyes.

'What is it? Was that too much of a compliment?' Mark asked, smiling back.

'Oh, be quiet,' she said, laughing.

Mark looked at her hands as she put the paintings back in the envelope. He thought about the feeling of holding her hand and wanted to hold it again.

A voice in the distance interrupted his thoughts. A low, almost guttural chant reached them through the thickets. Mark thought the voice sounded familiar, and he was right: after a few seconds, Oak emerged into the clearing.

He seemed perfectly oblivious to the world around him. The old man was pacing the grass with a wooden staff in his hand and chanting:

'The God is young. His strength is growing day by day, and there's fire in his arms, his sinews, and his loins. Where he steps, the ground gives way and water rushes in, filling lakes. Where he breathes out, the wind makes the leaves rustle and bends blades of grass. Where he waves his arms, a storm bends and breaks trees. The rain bathes his face and the wind ruffles his hair. Soon he will find the one who will take all his strength. He is travelling through the icy water and his journey is full of perils, and the God fears them for it was not he who created the water and the creatures that inhabit it.'

'Who's that?' Tandi asked, looking at him.

'His name's Oak,' Mark said. 'Well, that's the name everyone knows him by. He hasn't told anyone his real name – not since he moved to Birmingham. He's a bit… strange. Thinks he's a Celtic druid or something. He lives on my street.'

'He looks… creepy,' Tandi said.

'He's harmless.'

'Poor man. Has he always been like that?'

'People say he hasn't. He used to work in a bank, made tons of money. He's probably still living off it since he needs to buy bread and things.'

The old man took a knife out of his pocket and bent down to cut some herbs growing by the roots of an old tree with gnarled branches. He put them in his bag and disappeared down the path into the forest. Mark's gaze followed the old man. And then…

No, it couldn't be.

Where Oak's white robe had just been, there was another white garment. Overalls. Slick black extensions on the limbs. The horse was staring at him with unblinking eyes. They were dark like the craters of Mount Doom in Tandi's painting.

'*Flesh… eat my flesh,*' the horse whispered. The inside of its mouth was black. Its voice was cold and piercing like wintry wind.

Mark blinked. The vision disappeared.

'What is it?' Tandi asked.

'Nothing,' Mark replied. 'Thought I saw something.'

'Let's go,' she said, standing up. 'I haven't shown you the Shire Country Park yet.'

As they were walking back towards the road, Mark thought about Tandi's reaction to Oak. It seemed that she wanted to leave the sunlit meadow as soon as possible after seeing him. Perhaps she'd never seen someone like that. Mark was quite used to him since they were neighbours. Still, Tandi looked far too worried. He wondered why…

Part Two

June – July

Chapter 12

George

George could not sleep again and was angry with himself about it. He twisted and turned next to Sarah, who was deeply submerged in her dreams, and the repeated creaking of the old bedsprings could not wake her up.

The fact that he couldn't fall asleep was not the only thing that made George angry. Something strange was happening to him and he didn't like it one bit. He would not be able to tell anyone about it, that was for sure! It had been more than a month since he had had that conversation with the man in the mirror, and, whether it was real or not, he could not get it out of his mind. The very thought of the ridiculousness of it all made him cringe. How bloody mad was that! So he, a healthy man, was hearing voices and having visions now. What would happen next? A detailed doctor's report and a chamber with padded walls?

A plastic, oily flavour of disgust formed in George's mouth. He clenched his teeth awkwardly and bit his cheek. The metallic taste of blood made him nauseous. The memories of his sister Celia growing limp in his arms came back to haunt him and swarmed around him like annoying flies. He shook his head, got up, stumbled barefoot towards his bathroom and spat into the toilet bowl.

'Don't forget to flush,' said the voice in the mirror. George spun on the spot and swore. The familiar figure in pearly-white clothes lifted its forelimbs and slowly and methodically took off the horse's mask with dark, captivating eyes. George stared at the man: he had a different face this time. Short, dark hair. A small beard.

'I knew you would come back, George,' said the figure as it took human shape.

'Of course I would come back, Einstein,' George retorted. 'It's my bathroom, damn it! I will come back here every time I need to use it. Or perhaps I should go somewhere else, because the mirror is saying hello, and the next thing I know, the toilet will start begging me not to take a dump in it!'

'Ah, sarcasm – the best weapon of a gentleman!' the man said with a smile. 'But your barbed responses don't bother me, George. I'm very patient and persistent. I want us to have a proper conversation.'

'Well, Mister "Patient and Persistent",' said George, getting annoyed at the stranger's nonchalance, 'how can we have a conversation if I don't even know your name? You know mine, so it's not quite fair.'

'All right, I can do that. You can call me Rahab, but that doesn't mean much to you, I think.'

'Ray-hab?' George repeated, as if tasting the unfamiliar word in his mouth. 'What kind of name is that?'

'It's a name from a book,' the man in the mirror replied. 'A very old and good book.'

George didn't move and kept staring at the man who called himself Rahab. He had a strange feeling that he'd seen him somewhere before. The way his lips moved when he spoke, the tiny wrinkles in the corners of his eyes… he tried to remember where the feeling of familiarity came from, but it evaded him as soon as he tried to grasp the end of the thread of his thought.

As if guessing his thoughts, Rahab spoke:

'You're looking at me as if we've met before.'

'Of course,' George said in a drawling voice, pretending that the most obvious thing had just dawned on him. 'I meet sick and twisted folks like yourself every day. Every other one wears a fucking horse mask. What a load of bullshit!'

'Bullshit?' Rahab repeated. 'George, you're a funny guy! Your attitude is like a mask with holes that you've put on askew. I can still see your face, your eyes give you away. I will remind you, then. You have totally forgotten the face, but you might remember the words: *Water is a dangerous thing, George. You can watch the way it flows infinitely but it can very easily put a spell on you and make you forget where you are.*'

George stared at the man standing opposite him.

'How the hell do you know?' he whispered. He remembered now. He was ten years old, it was early spring and the winter that year was a very cold one. A thick layer of ice covered the water in the brook next to his home – he lived in Yorkshire back then. He was walking along the bank, watching floes break away from the large, white expanse and float away, melting in the rippling stream. Something attracted his attention and he bent down to look more closely at the water. All of a sudden, his head spun, the world went head over heels, the steep bank slipped from under his feet and he felt the cold water sting his face and soak his clothes, making them heavy and restricting his movement.

The brook was not that deep, but the slippery silt and seaweed on the stones at the bottom prevented him from standing up. He had swallowed a couple of pints of water and was spluttering and struggling to cling to the muddy bank, but the sodden clothes dragged him down and the current carried him further and further away. The soaked sleeves were heavy and wouldn't let him swim properly. This was the first time he really thought he was going to die. Fear paralysed him for a few moments; he struggled even to find enough breath to scream for help. Next, he started flailing his arms, whipping the water, trying to do something, anything as panic seized him.

And then he heard a splash next to him and felt a pair of strong arms hoist him up and carry him towards the bank. And there was a voice. A calm, measured voice telling him, 'Don't be afraid, lad. It's gonna be alright. You're safe. You're safe now.' The man had a car. He took him there, turned up the heating and told him to take off all his sodden clothes. He gave George a huge warm jumper and a blanket to wrap himself in, and took him home to his mother and stepfather. And while he was driving, he talked about water. Using the very same words.

Water is a dangerous thing, George. You can watch the way it flows infinitely but it can very easily put a spell on you and make you forget where you are.

He wanted to doubt it. He wanted to reject it, but he could not. He remembered the words too clearly. He had never told anyone about these words. He alone heard them that day.

'It was you,' George said, flatly. 'You saved me.'

Rahab nodded and said:

'You were just too young and too frightened to remember.'

Suddenly, the taps in the bathroom opened by themselves and water started filling the bathtub, overflowing onto the floor, rising higher and higher. George dashed towards the taps to close them, but slipped on the wet floor, fell flat on his back and woke with a start in his bed.

For a while, he lay still, listening to the sounds in the dark. Sarah's peaceful breathing. The ticking of the cheap alarm clock on the bedside table. The distant hum of night traffic; a car buzzing past like a lonely fly, then silence.

And suddenly he remembered where else he had seen the man in the mirror. The realisation came to him so abruptly, as if someone had pulled a plug out of the bathtub, letting out the soapy water full of suds. His mind was clear, and the realisation was scary.

George remembered that day. He was kneeling. Tears were streaming down his face. Angry red stripes marked the backs of his thighs. He saw…

The same man, the one in the mirror…

No, this wasn't possible! He was surely going mad.

George slept very badly that night.

Chapter 13

Mark

Mark looked at Tandi's hands as they drew ornaments in paint on a wooden toolbox he'd made this morning.

'You're good,' he said, 'I must admit it. I can only paint walls using a huge brush. Can't do fine strokes like you do.'

'I can't make things out of wood,' Tandi replied. 'Everyone's talents are different. By the way,' she added, 'you promised me you'd show me some of the books your grandpa made.'

'Oh, yes,' Mark said. It had been a fortnight since their visit to Sarehole Mill. They had been to a couple of different places around Birmingham since then, but hadn't been to his factory until today. Mark stood up and went into the corner of the workshop. He lifted the edge of the old carpet. There was a trapdoor underneath it with another padlock on it.

Mark took the set of keys from around his neck and unlocked it. Tandi looked inside curiously. There was a small wooden chest inside a foot-deep niche. Mark lifted the chest out and opened it. There were several leather-bound books inside. Mark took one out randomly. There was nothing on the cover.

'Come on, open it!' Tandi said. Mark flipped the leather cover open. Tandi's eyes widened. Inside, there was another cover, a wooden one. A thin rectangle made of yellow wood had the title intricately carved into it.

The Hobbit, or There and Back Again by J. R. R. Tolkien. Illustrated by Christopher McRae.

The letters were framed by a carved ornament of oak leaves. Mark lifted the wooden cover and saw Tandi's amazement grow.

'It's handwritten,' she whispered. 'Just like in the old days.'

The entire book was copied in Mark's grandfather's neat handwriting and illustrated in coloured ink. There were pictures of the elves and dwarves, the Lonely Mountain topped with darkening clouds and the dragon circling its menacing peak.

'It's really something, isn't it?' Mark said.

'Yes, it's incredible. Especially the covers.'

'Yeah, I wish I could do something like that,' Mark said.

'Practice makes perfect,' Tandi replied. 'That's what my dad told me many times.'

Suddenly Tandi became serious.

'Mark,' she said, turning to him, 'I wanted to tell you something. But you've got to promise me you won't get offended.'

Mark looked back at her in amazement. This was so unlike the Tandi he knew – she usually threw jibes at him without ever bothering to check if she was sensitive enough. Not that he minded, though – he liked the fact that she was so outspoken and sincere. When she made jokes about him, he felt she trusted him. If you can make a joke about someone, it means you consider them a friend.

'Yes,' he began, hesitantly. 'What is it?'

'Promise me, please.' He could feel that she was nervous for some reason.

'I promise I won't get offended,' he said. 'What is it?'

'Mark…' She bit her lip. 'I've been listening to what you've been telling me about your family. I've noticed one thing – you talk about your grandpa a lot, but you don't mention your parents very often. I feel that… correct me if I'm wrong, but I feel you don't talk to them too much. You've not told me about any recent conversations or activities you have done together. If you do talk about them, you talk in the past tense, about things that happened a long time ago, like things you did in the past with your dad. I think you should talk to your parents more often – at least tell them how your day went. For example, do they know you've got a new friend called Tandi?'

Mark did not expect this question. He started feeling very awkward.

'I haven't told them,' he admitted.

'Why? Have they been arguing?'

'No, it's not that... they're arguing less. My dad stopped drinking. Things are... I suppose they're more okay than they used to be.'

'So what's the problem?'

'It's Dad,' Mark said. 'Something's happening to him, something I can't explain or understand,' he added, shaking his head. 'He's changed and I can't understand this change. He's become silent, more reserved. He used to be different – you know, outgoing, liked a good laugh. He's always been a good sport, Dad has. When I was a kid, we used to have newspaper fights on the couch in the living room in the evenings. Mum was always telling us not to be so loud. He used to take me to the woods as well – just the two of us, just the lads as he called it, you know. He knows quite a lot about animals for someone who's been living in cities all his life. But now he's just so silent and secretive all the time.'

Mark fell silent. Somehow, talking about it made him feel better. At least he was able to comprehend the problem, if not the solution – and talking to Tandi as opposed to anyone else made a lot of difference as well. She was a strict listener, though, and did not relent.

'Have you thought that if you spoke to your dad – both your parents, in fact – you'd be able to understand each other better? Perhaps you should share your thoughts with your parents. You told me the day we met that you were tired of them arguing and you felt they paid no attention to you. Maybe you only said it because you were angry, but perhaps they also feel neglected because you're not telling them anything?'

Mark didn't know what to answer to that. He wanted to defend himself, but the arguments didn't come. He wanted to feel offended, but could not force himself to – either because it was Tandi speaking to him or because he'd promised her he wouldn't, or because, deep down, he knew that she was right.

'And what about you?' he asked finally, turning to her.

'Me?' she repeated.

'Yes. Do your parents know you've got a new friend? And what do they say to that?'

Tandi became even more serious. Suddenly Mark had an impression that she looked much older.

'I'm sure my parents know, but they say nothing to that. My parents are dead, Mark.'

This was the last thing Mark had expected to hear. During all this time, during their every meeting, Tandi would mention something about her family, but he never paid attention to the fact that most of her stories were also in the past tense. Everything that she said about her family, except for her aunt, went along the lines of 'my dad once said' or 'my mum once did'. Of course! Now, as she said it, everything fell into place and was so obvious. What a fool he'd been!

Mark thought he should say something, but every sentence started to sound stupid before he had even finished formulating it. Tandi spared his embarrassment by talking first:

'They both died in a car crash,' she said quietly but clearly. 'I was eight years old. They went to some work-related event in Manchester, and they were thinking of taking me as well, but all of a sudden I fell ill – you know, like kids do – and they left me with my aunt. They never even reached their destination – another car crashed into theirs. They died on the spot, and so did the other driver. Of course, he was drunk. So I have the same reason to hate it when people drink.'

'And now you're living with your aunt.'

'Yes, with her. We take good care of each other – she's quite old and is losing her eyesight. She says she's okay with glasses, but maybe she's just saying that to make me less worried.'

'I'm sorry to hear that,' Mark muttered, looking at Tandi. 'About your aunt. And your parents.' He was really embarrassed, and felt that it had been horribly tactless to say what he had said to her earlier. 'I just... I never knew, never made the connection.'

'I know you didn't,' Tandi said, calmly. 'It's the way I speak about them. I know they're gone, that they aren't coming back and I don't speak about them in the present, as if they were alive. But I believe they are watching over me, keeping me safe, and I talk about them all the time to, like, honour their memory. I believe that as long as you are remembered, you are never really gone. You live on, in the hearts of the people you love, and who love you.'

'That's a beautiful thought,' Mark said. 'You know, it was my grandfather who taught me about wood carving. We were quite close, you know. Every time I pick up a knife, I remember him. I hope I keep his memory alive in the things I make – like, in the people, animals and plants I make out of wood.'

'Yes, it's exactly like that,' Tandi said. 'Do you have anything else here that was made by him?'

Mark stood up and walked towards a large object in the corner of the workshop covered with a case made of cloth. He lifted the cover and heard Tandi gasp. Inside, there was an upright piano. Every side of it was covered in carvings. The front depicted a sleepy village with a river running through it. Tiny houses nestled on the left side with a church spire towering over them. A forest stood on the right with animals and birds visible among the trees.

In silence, Tandi lifted the keyboard cover and played a few notes. The sounds hung sheepishly in the air for a few moments, and then a more harmonious melody emerged. Mark looked at the dark skin of Tandi's hands that stood out against the ivory keys in the semi-darkness of the room. All her feistiness was gone; he could see that she was concentrating on the keyboard, and even Spot had calmed down and seemed to be listening to the music that was coming from under his mistress's hands. This girl kept surprising him. What else was she good at?

'You play well,' Mark noted, turning to Tandi. She smiled shyly.

'Thank you. But there are people who play better. I haven't been practising enough.'

'It reminds me of my mum,' she added after a brief pause. 'She used to play the piano. Much better than I do.'

'Was she a musician? I mean, professionally?'

'No,' Tandi replied, 'she wasn't. She earned her living as a nurse. But my grandfather wanted all of the children in his family to develop a talent, like learning a language or an instrument. So she was taught how to play the piano.

'Mum used to work in a very rough place – a prison infirmary. My aunt has told me a lot about her. I really admire her, you know. She didn't care how rude those men in the prison were, or what they were doing their time for. She just carried on with her job. And what was more – she seemed to genuinely like those guys. A lot of them weren't so bad if you scratched the surface.'

'You seem to have inherited that from your mother,' Mark said.

'What exactly?'

'Well, for a start, you pay no attention to rudeness.'

'It's nice to know I'm like her in some way,' Tandi said.

'And what about your dad,' Mark asked. 'What did he do?'

'My dad also worked in a hospital,' Tandi said. 'He did clinical trials. You know, like blood tests and all that.'

'What did he think about your mum working in such a dangerous place?'

'He thought that all lives are worth saving.'

Mark nodded. He and Tandi looked at one another. This was their first serious conversation since they had first met.

'Thank you,' Tandi said.

'For what?'

'For being the person I can talk to about it. I've been keeping this inside me for too long.'

'Thank you, too,' Mark said. 'For listening to me and for paying no attention to my rudeness that day.'

'That's what friends are for, right?' Tandi answered, smiling.

'Talk to your parents,' she added. 'Especially your dad.'

'I will,' Mark promised.

Chapter 14

Sarah

'A little shorter at the back, I think', Sarah said, putting the tape measure on the table. She had been adjusting one of the dresses that Jo had ordered from her.

'Yes, I think so, too,' Jo said, smiling. 'You're a real expert. You should do this full-time, you know.'

Sarah blushed at the praise.

'Thank you, Jo,' she said. 'The work I do with my own hands means a lot to me. Actually, more than the secretarial work I do in the office. I'm very happy I work part-time – this way, I can squeeze in some time for sewing.'

'I could recommend you to some people,' Jo said. 'Maybe you'll be able to do more of it. Let's take a break, shall we,' she suggested. 'I can smell your lovely cake from here.'

'I'll make coffee,' Sarah said. 'But I'd like to make it your way. What do you add to it to make it smell and taste so… special?'

'Oh, it's very easy, love. You just add a pinch of cinnamon and a little bit of ground ginger. Come, I'll show you.'

They went to the kitchen to make coffee. Sarah was happy that this time they had been able to meet at her place and not at Jo's – she didn't need to bring all her fabrics with her. George was away, busy with a building project in the North West; Mark was out in the city – he had probably wandered off to explore another neighbourhood he'd not been to yet.

The women returned to the living room of the Davies' house with coffee and cake on a tray. Sarah picked up her thick-sided mug, inhaled the smell and smiled.

'It smells like it's Christmas,' she said, dreamily. 'Christmas in the middle of summer.'

The smell reminded her of every Christmas in her life – her childhood years at the orphanage, when the children opened large boxes sent by local charities and churches; lonely and cold winters on council estates in Walsall and Wolverhampton as she tried to catch up with all the opportunities she'd not had before: get a job, justify all the hard work she had put in for her GCSEs, get off the dole, meet a decent guy…

The year she met George, she was an independent woman with a secondary school certificate and a job as a sales assistant. She had even taken up an evening course in clothes making and was hoping to earn a bit on the side as a seamstress – the trade she had learnt the basics of at the orphanage. Her and George's first Christmas together at his parents' home was there, in her memory, as well. A simple working family, so friendly and sincere – and the smell of Christmas coffee, with cinnamon in it, too.

'I'm glad to see you smiling,' Jo said. 'You look very pretty when you smile.'

'Thank you,' Sarah said, blushing again. 'Things are better now between me and George. He's stopped drinking. I'm happy he realised the harm he was doing to himself – and to our family. He's become closer to the family. He's talking to Mark more as well. By the way, speaking of him – I know school's over now, but how's he been doing in the last few weeks?'

Jo hesitated for a moment.

'Not too badly,' she said. 'One positive thing teachers have noticed is that he's become more outgoing; he's talked more to his classmates, made jokes… I've been able to see this very positive change. On the other hand, he used to look as if he was daydreaming in the past, but if you asked him something, he would always respond. Over the past few weeks, though, he really was daydreaming. It looked as if he lacked concentration. Must have had something to do with the coming holidays.'

'Or not,' Sarah said, smiling even more. 'I think I know what the reason for that might be. I've noticed he's been paying more attention to his appearance and clothes than usual – you know, stuck in the bathroom, grooming himself. I think there might be a girl on the horizon.'

Jo's eyes livened up.

'Really?' she said. 'You think so?'

'Yep,' Sarah said, nodding. 'And if so, I think it's doing him a lot of good. He's helping around the house, he helps me carry my shopping without me asking him to. He's learning how to treat a lady. He's really growing into a fine young man, it seems to me,' she concluded and suddenly burst out laughing.

'What's the matter?' Jo asked.

'Well,' Sarah said, still laughing, 'it's the way you leant towards me as I was talking. I really felt as if we were a pair of gossiping teenage girls! Except the gossip is even more interesting because it's about my own son.'

Jo also laughed at the thought of them being two gossipy giggly girls again.

'It's true, though,' Sarah continued. 'Mark's been going out quite a lot and not telling me or George exactly where he was going. He did that in the past – especially when George was drinking. But it's different now, somehow – I can feel he's not going off to roam the streets.'

'I know what you mean, love,' Jo said. 'I had a feeling like that when my own little ones went out without telling me where. It was quite funny, though – them trying to hide the real reason for their disappearance,' she added with a chuckle. 'At least you've got a son, so you can be less worried about him coming home late. I was much less concerned about my son than about my two girls. You're lucky not knowing what it's like to worry about your daughter.'

'Well,' Sarah said after a small hesitation, 'you never know. Maybe soon enough I'll be lucky to know.'

'What do you mean?' Jo said. Sarah took a deep breath, exhaled resolutely and said:

'Jo, I think I'm pregnant.'

A few seconds of silence followed.

'Are you sure?' Jo asked finally.

'I… don't know. I think so, I mean, I'm late. About six weeks late, actually. I haven't told anyone yet – not even George. I feel so nervous… and so stupid!'

'What do you feel stupid about?' Jo asked. 'There's nothing stupid about being pregnant. You look quite happy about it.'

'I am, Jo. It's just… we haven't been planning for a little one. It's all so unexpected. And I'm much older than I was when I had Mark.'

'Oh, cut it out, love! You're talking as if you were fifty. It's definitely not too late to have children at your age. I wasn't much younger than you are now when I had my youngest daughter. You'll be fine, you'll see.'

'I... I hope so,' said Sarah, blushing. 'George is away at the moment. He's in Liverpool, working on a construction project. I'm going to tell him as soon as he comes back. Make a nice dinner, you know, that kind of thing.'

'You do that,' Jo said. 'I think he'll be very happy to hear this news.'

'I'm sure he will,' Sarah said. 'Still, it's just so... so sudden and unexpected.'

Jo moved towards her and put her hands on Sarah's shoulders.

'Dear, do you remember yourself when you had Mark?'

'Yes,' Sarah answered, not sure what Jo was getting at.

'Was that sudden and unexpected too?'

'Well... it was. But both George and I wanted children, so it was a very pleasant surprise.'

'Is the surprise unpleasant this time?'

'What are you saying, of course it's pleasant!'

'Do you not want the baby?'

'Of course I want...' Sarah paused, not wanting to say 'it'. 'Her... or him,' she added.

'So what's the problem? Stop worrying about it. I'm sure your husband will be so excited about the news! When is he coming back?'

'Tomorrow.'

'Then I won't disturb you much longer. You need time to prepare. Let's finish measuring this dress quickly and I'll leave you to it.'

Chapter 15

George

George was kneeling before a painting of Jesus. White, almost bluish light was pouring out of the wounds in His palms and heart. In the heart, another beam joined it, dangerously, angrily scarlet. Just as scarlet as the backs of his legs, where he had been hit with the belt. The floor was hard and uncomfortable; his bare knees hurt, making him wince in pain, but he dared not move or make a sound.

The man standing behind him stepped forward towards him. George felt trembling hollowness spread in his chest and stomach.

'Repeat after me!' the authoritative voice barked above him. 'Say: my Lord and God, I accept this punishment.'

'My Lord and God, I acc-accept this pu-punishment,' George repeated. Something was sticking in his throat; everything inside him was shivering and the hollowness swelled, stealing space in his lungs, making him stutter.

'And I am grateful for it because I deserved it.'

'And I am grateful f-for it bec-because I deser-deserved it.'

Slap!

Fire shot through his ear. The light pouring from Jesus' wounds became blurred and shimmered as tears welled up in his eyes.

'Stop mumbling like some idiot!' the voice snapped. 'Speak loudly and clearly!'

George wiped the tears and mucus with the sleeve of his pyjamas and repeated the words, breathing after every three or four words, trying not to stutter.

'And I promise never to be late home again,' his father continued.

George repeated the sentence in a trembling voice. The frightened hollowness resurged and a lump in his throat hurt unbearably. He needed to cry out to make the pain go away, but he had to swallow the scream, fearing a new beating.

'Now kiss my hand.' The rough, hairy hand with short and stubby fingers shot in his direction. The boy recoiled instinctively — even this gesture carried the threat of a punch or a slap. He touched the skin that reeked disgustingly of tobacco with his lips.

'That's the way,' the voice barked. 'That's what the Good Book says. Folly is bound up in the heart of a child, but the rod of discipline will drive it far from him. *Now, George, look up at our Lord and Saviour and say The Lord's Prayer ten times. Slowly and with respect.'*

George looked up at the face of Jesus and froze in horror. The familiar image with light and sorrow in His eyes was gone. Instead, there was a white long face of a horse with eyes as black as the darkest secrets of the Universe. It smiled, showing its huge rectangular teeth. Little George stared at it, transfixed, his lips whispering the words 'Our Father, who art in heaven...' almost automatically. The black eyes started expanding and George saw currents twisting within the pupils. The creature's eyes became two vortexes that were sucking in all the light in the room until darkness consumed him completely...

George gasped and woke up. He sat up and his eyes darted around the room, looking at the walls and ceiling. He was not at home but at a hostel on the outskirts of Liverpool overlooking the canal. He'd come here for a building project – a very short one, just four days.

Moonlight was pouring through the window: he'd forgotten to close the curtains. George got up and went to the bathroom, leant over the sink, splashed some water on his face, and sat on the edge of the bathtub.

It had been a while since he last had this dream. He had even forgotten all the details – after all, his violent, drunken father had disappeared from his life a long time ago. He remembered how, when he was ten years old, he dreamt about this bizarre transformation of Jesus in the painting for the first time. Then the dream returned a few more times, but he had never understood the meaning of the transformation. Until now.

Now, the same face was staring at him from the mirror.

'I knew you would be back looking for me, Georgie Porgie,' the horse said.

George froze at the sound of the name the being in the mirror had just called him. It was a special name his stepfather used to call him. No one else knew that name. He'd never told it to anyone except Sarah.

'How do you know?' he asked. 'Who are you?'

The horse took off its head-mask again and turned into a young man. The familiar face: long hair, a small beard. So much sorrow and darkness in his eyes... the sorrow and darkness of knowledge.

'Who the hell are you?' George repeated. 'And what do you want?'

He turned his gaze away from the mirror but he knew that the man was there, staring at him, a smile shining through his eyes. This smile made George feel uncomfortable: somehow it evoked his best and worst memories at the same time.

'I have many names, Georgie. One of them is Rahab, as I mentioned, and you are free to use it if you like.'

'Ray-hab,' George repeated, looking straight before himself. 'What's this name?'

'As I told you before, it is a name that comes from an ancient and beautiful language in which one particularly influential book was written. You know this book, Georgie Porgie, because you were taught to respect and honour it as a child, by two different people. Both of them have the right to be called your father, but for very different reasons.'

Rahab held a long pause. Slowly, George lifted his eyes towards the mirror.

'I recognise these eyes,' Rahab said. 'You looked at me with the same eyes before, remember?'

Something inside George's chest and stomach leapt suddenly. He *did* remember. What he had just seen in his dream was not a recent vision overlaying an old nightmare. He had seen it before, that evening when he came home ten minutes later than he was supposed to and his father beat him until red, angry stripes stood out against the pale skin of his legs. The same face, the face of a large-toothed horse, looked at him from the painting of Jesus on the wall. Only for a split second – he thought he'd imagined it – but now he knew it was real. It *did* happen. And, shit, it scared him now.

'Yes, Georgie Porgie, it was I who looked back at you.'

'Can you please stop using that name!' George said, turning away.

'Why? It was I who gave your stepdad the tongue in which he uttered it. I know your heart. You are afraid, I can see it – but have you not read the Scripture? What do I say all the time in it, George?'

'Repent and love your enemies?' George guessed in a hoarse voice.

'Not even close. *Fear not!* These are the words that echo through the centuries. I've always watched over you. I protected you even if you thought I'd abandoned you. It was I who gave your mother the courage to leave your violent father who used my teachings to spread evil around himself. It was I who brought Christopher McRae into your life – he became your stepfather and defied all the prejudice about stepfathers by showing you my Love and my Grace like no one before.'

George felt like his head was going to explode.

'I don't get this,' he said finally. 'If you are... Him, then how come your appearance...' he stopped, lost for words.

Rahab chuckled.

'And what did you want me to appear as? A burning bush? Or a handsome Italian-looking hippie from an Italian master's painting? I know you heart, George. This kind of appearance was the only one likely to draw your attention for I know how cold you have remained towards that vestige of your faith that you still carry inside yourself. Despite your stepfather's relentless efforts to show you that my ways are not your father's ways.'

George lowered his eyes and felt heat rise in his cheeks.

'But I don't blame you, Georgie Porgie,' Rahab continued. 'Your father is to blame. He always kept you in fear, he distorted and perverted my teachings, my Scripture. It was due to him that you've developed a crust on your soul and grown indifferent towards the Church. But you don't need either the Scripture or the Church because I want to make a home in another place – your soul. Together we can succeed where your stepfather has failed if you stop being stubborn and open up your heart. What say you?'

George stood silent, ashamed of the tears that were welling in his eyes. Suddenly he remembered his other dream, the one about the man who saved him from the icy river. A question formed in his mind, but it was so audacious that the very thought of asking it scared George. Yet, he had to know. His knees started trembling so violently, he thought his legs were going to give way. Finally, he swallowed hard and asked:

'Were you the same... The same man who pulled me out of the river?'

Rahab smiled.

'There's a reason why I'm called a Saviour.'

The trembling in George's knees spread through his entire body.

'Why me?' he asked finally. 'Why me, why now?'

'You have not chosen me, I have chosen you, Georgie Porgie. From now on, you won't even need a mirror to talk to me. You can talk to me any time if you choose to. But I have never forced anyone to accept me. I am standing at the door and knocking, and will come in only if you open. Will you open your door, George? Do you agree to let me in? What say you, George Davies?'

The man in the mirror smiled and extended his hand. George felt his head spin. Images flashed through his mind: his father's hand drawn back and ready to hit him; his stepfather's smiling face and large hands covered in calluses from physical labour gently washing his grazed knee; his mother's tears; the face of Jesus through which the horse mask shone, the hand of the man in the mirror blessing him, the dark eyes like vortexes that he was so drawn to...

Hearing his own voice as if through the mist, George uttered:

'I do.'

'Thank you,' the horse said and disappeared.

George went back into the room and sank onto his bed, burying his face in his hands. Memories flooded in, flashing through the fog in his mind that would not clear.

Rahab knew him as if he saw right through his heart. Could he really be… the One who had looked at him from the painting of Jesus that night? There was no other explanation. It must have been him all along.

George's relationship with his faith and God was a complicated one. His father had done a very good job of ruining it; he had a habit of using his belt and Bible verses at the same time. A man with a horrible temper who pretended to be a loving father and a family man at Sunday services. But all his love and kindness didn't even last as long as Sunday evening. He always found an excuse to beat his wife and son – it seemed that he actually *liked* it. Finally, after he broke her arm, George's mother plucked up her courage and kicked her husband out. Very soon, he was arrested for a brawl in a pub and then disappeared from their lives behind prison walls.

A couple of years later, George's mother married Christopher McRae – a man she met in church (the perfect place to meet a spouse, she used to say). Christopher McRae was more of a father than the Davies man. He showed George a very different picture of God and the Gospel. His message about faith was a message of love and forgiveness. He tried very hard to show that going to church was not a duty, but rather a right and a privilege. When George was not doing well at school, his stepfather's face darkened and he said, 'I won't take you to church with me this Sunday.'

Unlike George's real father, who thought that children should be grateful first and foremost for the punishment they receive, Christopher McRae had raised George to be grateful for everything good that happened in his life, no matter how small or insignificant it appeared. Yet, George's heart remained lukewarm. He went to Sunday services, took part in Holy Communion married in church and baptised Mark in church, but nothing could repair the damage done by his father's abusive education. Nothing in his soul moved – it was as if his inner world was deaf and did not hear the Call. Sometimes, when he spent time with his stepfather doing 'man things' like fishing or helping him in his workshop, he felt the need to talk about it and then something very weak stirred inside him, struggling to be expressed in words.

Tonight, he felt it again – stronger than ever. Something moved inside him during his conversation with Rahab. It was something private, something intimate he felt he could not share with anyone – not even with Sarah. Two emotions were fighting within him – on the one hand, he was almost ashamed to admit what he had just experienced; it was something that befitted meek and pious nuns, not healthy working-class men. On the other hand, that strange feeling seemed as real as anything – and he treasured it and didn't want to let it go.

'You're not going bonkers, George,' Rahab suddenly said. 'You're discovering a new world. A place you've never been before.'

'But…' George paused, trying to think how to formulate the question better. 'I just wanted to know… Why did you start talking to me? I mean, I'm no saint, I'm not a prophet or anything. I'm… I've been a very angry man recently. Why?'

'It shows that you didn't read the Scripture. If you had, you would know that I don't look for holiness. I look for loyalty – pause to think about it, Georgie Porgie.'

He held a long pause, as if to allow the message to really sink in.

'And about anger…' Rahab continued, 'Anger in itself is not a bad thing. In fact, it's my gift to you. The most important thing is to know what to direct your anger at. You can get angry at something that pulls you away from me. You can get angry at a person who wants to take what you have from you – and you have the right to shut that person up. Not only is it your right, but it is also your duty. The duty of a faithful and loyal friend.

'Now I will leave you alone, George. But if you ever need reassurance or advice, just call my name. I will be there for you. Always.'

George collapsed onto his bed.

'Thank you,' he whispered into the darkness.

The blackened mouth of the horse looked like a distant galaxy. It attracted him, pulled him towards itself, becoming larger and larger until it swallowed him. George heard someone whisper: *eat my flesh… drink my blood* and realised he was dreaming.

That night, he slept better than he had ever slept in his life.

Chapter 16

Sarah

Sarah's hands shook a little as she ran them down the starched tablecloth and lay cutlery on the table. Tonight she would prepare a special dinner and tell George she was expecting.

'I don't get it,' Mary Beth said, jumping onto the table and swinging her legs off the edge. 'Why are you so nervous?'

'I don't know,' Sarah said. 'I just don't know how George will react.'

'Jo's already told you – he'll be happy. You'll spend time together, just the two of you – just like in the good old days.'

That was true – she missed those days. Mark had gone out – he had told her he'd be in George's stepfather's old workshop. She wondered whether he'd gone alone or if the girl he was seeing was there too. She still hadn't found a convenient moment to talk to him about it. Well, truth be told, she didn't even know how to talk to her son about these things. No one had talked to her about it – she had had to find it all out from life experience. Books that could have been useful were published after she'd given birth to Mark, and all the knowledge had become more or less irrelevant.

'And what's the problem anyway?' Mary Beth asked, playing with a shiny fork. 'Being pregnant in your thirties is better than in your teens!'

'Late thirties,' Sarah corrected.

'Big deal!' Mary Beth retorted. 'Are you feeling bad? Is something wrong?'

'No, nothing's wrong. It's…' Sarah paused, 'it's quite surprising, actually.'

Sarah listened to her body. Somehow her pregnancy made her feel younger, more alive, more active. That felt… strange and almost unnatural. When she had been pregnant with Mark, it was quite tiring. He'd given her a lot of trouble: morning sickness that could be triggered by anything, anytime. Suddenly, she could no longer stand the smells she used to love – like burning incense in church or even something as commonplace as fried eggs. And she was feeling so tired all the time! Yet this time, every morning as she woke up, she felt full of energy and as ready to face the new day as she'd ever felt before. And there was no morning sickness whatsoever – well, maybe she felt a little nauseous every now and again, but there was nothing that would prevent her from doing everyday activities as usual.

She actually couldn't believe how special it felt. Really, she was going to be a mother, again!

'It's just… well, you know… everything at once,' she said, turning to Mary Beth. 'I'm a little overwhelmed.'

'I can understand that,' Mary Beth said. 'But I still see no reason to be so nervous.'

'I guess,' she admitted, 'I'm also worried about Mark. I think he's seeing a girl, and well…'

'Your own pregnancy is making you wonder if they've had sex already,' Mary Beth finished for her. Sarah nodded. Her 'mother and wife's gut feeling' that she had learnt to trust over the years couldn't give her the slightest idea about Mark's private life. Apparently, it was meant to remain private.

'I just have no idea how to broach the subject,' she admitted. 'You remember what it was like at the orphanage.'

'Yes, both Sister Grey and Sister Margaret were equally strict about it.'

Sarah remembered that really well. Sisters Grey and Margaret were the nuns assigned to the group of girls to which Sarah belonged. They were responsible for their education. Both the overly stern Sister Grey and the smiley, gentle Sister Margaret adopted the same strict tone when they talked about boys. There was nothing easier than getting pregnant, they said, and all boys wanted nothing more than to get inside a girl's knickers.

'That kind of education kept you out of trouble, didn't it?' Mary Beth remarked.

'Yes, it did,' Sarah agreed. 'But it didn't work for everyone. And if I had a teenage daughter, I wouldn't know how to approach this topic with her.'

'I think you're overcomplicating things,' Mary Beth said, jumping off the table. 'George is leaving for Scotland for a few days in a week's time, isn't he? It's a perfect chance for you to catch your son and speak to him, eye to eye.'

'Perhaps it would be better if George talked to him about it? You know, man-to-man, lads only? Or should both of us be there?'

'What exactly do you want to tell Mark?' Mary Beth asked.

'How to treat a woman. How to be a good boyfriend.'

'And don't you think that a woman should tell her son how to treat a woman?'

'You're right,' Sarah said, nodding in agreement. She thought so herself, but she was happy to hear that Mary Beth's opinion was the same.

'Stop worrying and continue preparing,' Mary Beth ordered. 'George is almost here.'

Sarah took a deep breath and resolutely marched upstairs into the bedroom to change into something pretty and attractive. Whatever George's reaction would be, looking her best was never a bad strategy.

Chapter 17

George

George went to the bathroom to take a shower and catch his breath. He deliberately let the water cool and stepped into the bathtub, letting the water wash over him like refreshing rain after a sweltering day. He stuck his head under the hissing streams and shook it like a dog, spluttering with pleasure, thoroughly enjoying the feeling. He needed to cool down after having just made love to his wife three times in a row. He felt as if he'd just lost twenty pounds and become fifteen years younger.

The coolness of the water reminded him of the brook where he used to play with the local boys when he was a child. Oh, he would love to jump into that brook together with Sarah, naked, away from everyone's prying eyes. He imagined her growing belly and felt he was getting aroused again.

'I can't believe she's pregnant,' he whispered.

'And how do you feel about it?'

This time, George did not jump when he heard Rahab's voice. He had expected him to come and, in fact, wanted to talk to him.

'I'm happy,' he said, smiling. 'Really happy. It's great news. My gun's been missing the target since Mark was born and now – look at me, bullseye again!'

'I'm happy for you too, George,' Rahab said. 'It looks like you've still got power in both your arms and your loins. Your wife must be pleased,' he added with laddish bravado.

'I think she is, and I'll happily please her again,' George replied with a feisty grin. He began to feel really relaxed around Rahab, like he was just one of the lads to whom he could tell just about anything – and yet, he felt somehow special and privileged. Rahab understood him like no one else did. It was as if they thought the same way.

'It's the news, Rahab,' he explained, turning on the hot water, lathering himself with soap and scrubbing with a rough sponge. 'About the baby. I'm very excited, but I know it'll change our lives again. We're not as young as we were when Mark was born, but I think we'll manage with experience now. And I think cutting down on drinking helped my manhood as well.'

'I suppose it did,' Rahab said. 'And what do your buddies say now that you've stopped going out with them?'

Did George imagine it, or did he hear disappointment in Rahab's voice?

'I'm a family man,' he said, trying not to sound apologetic. 'I don't just do what I want, I also do what needs to be done. If they are my real friends, they'll understand that.'

'Fair enough, George, fair enough,' Rahab said and sighed. George felt something was wrong but couldn't understand what the matter was. All he was trying to do was spend more time with his family and treat them right.

'George, I see that you feel annoyed now,' Rahab said. 'I'm not telling you to think in extremes. It's not either your friends or your family, it's not a winners and losers situation. It's life, and it's possible to have a balance. Just don't forget your friends. Or perhaps I wanted to say: don't forget… me.'

Rahab's face appeared in the steamed-up mirror. George could see it from behind the shower curtain. He wiped the steamed-up glass and looked into the man's eyes, dark as the waters of the canal at night. Rahab's words startled him.

'I… I never meant it like this. You're the first one I'm sharing the news about the baby with! I won't forget you. I can't forget you. You're the only one who understands me. My mates… well, they're mates. There are things I can't share with them! We're friends – real friends, right?' he added, suddenly feeling embarrassed.

To his surprise, Rahab burst into a hearty laugh.

'Of course we are! Closest ever.'

'Right,' George said, feeling relieved. Damn it, talking to Rahab was complicated. But talking to him added something new to his life, new qualities he hadn't known about before. He had to admit it to himself: he was afraid of losing his new friend now. No matter how busy the new baby would keep him, he'd need to find time to talk to Rahab.

'There was something else I wanted to tell you, George. Something we must talk about.'

George got out of the shower and started drying himself with a towel.

'What is it?' There was unsettling seriousness in Rehab's voice.

'I am afraid your wife's pregnancy might complicate things. There's... there's a competitor.'

'What do you mean?'

'Someone who wants to share your wife's attention.'

George felt something icy and slippery slide down his back.

'Who is it?' he asked, his voice wooden.

'So far, it's no one. Your wife does not recognise the signals he's sending her. She is yours. For now,' he added pointedly.

'Who is this... this bastard?' George asked. 'Has he made any passes at my wife yet?'

'I can't tell you, George. I can only tell you what I know about your heart, not someone else's. This is not only about you, but also about your wife. You can only trust what she's telling you... and your own instincts. As usual, I can only advise you.'

George felt hope spreading inside him like a hot drink, melting away the icy feeling that had been building up in his throat.

'What can you advise me?'

'To be careful. To be watchful. To pay attention to small things. I've warned you. Do you trust me?'

'Always,' George said, feeling the warmth wash over him.

'The enemy is real. You have to take control of the situation. And you will. Sarah is yours. Yours alone.'

'*Yours.*'

The last word was whispered right into George's ear. He felt the soft breath on his skin. Someone was standing behind him. He felt a pair of tender hands wrap around his waist. There was a woman behind him. He turned to face her: she had black hair with streaks of red glowing like embers that ran down her shoulders, cloaking her naked body.

'Don't be scared, George,' she said, looking into his eyes. 'I am just another face of the One you already know.'

'This is Lilith, George,' Rahab said. 'Say hello.' George felt a bolt of current flash down his stomach, the pulsating blood swelling his desire.

'Remember,' the woman whispered, 'she should not know you suspect anything. Act like you know nothing. And now go and show your wife you own her. Have her now, with full force.'

Then she disappeared, but the image of her slender, muscular body was burned into George's mind. He stepped out of the bathroom and headed for the bedroom. Sarah was his, and only his. Nobody would take her from him. He would stop it. He would stop *her* if need be.

He opened the bedroom door; Sarah was lying on her stomach, her legs slightly open. He walked to her and grabbed her by the hips.

'George!' she exclaimed in surprise. 'Did you come back for more?'

'Oh yes, I did!' he whispered, pressing her close to himself. He would have her with full force, all right – like there was no tomorrow!

Chapter 18

Mark

Mark walked up the path lined with small, flat stones and looked around. He was standing at the top of Bilberry Hill in the Lickey Hills Country Park. The park was situated on the border between two counties – the West Midlands and Worcestershire. The countryside with rolling hills and a dark green pine forest could be seen in the distance on the left. The skyline of the city of Birmingham could be seen on the right: the tall spire of the BT Tower and the white and brown blocks of flats around it, protruding into the sky, towering over the terraced and semi-detached houses. A large reservoir gleamed like a mirror at the bottom of the hill, reflecting the sky with a few scattered clouds.

'Nice view, eh?' said his father coming behind him.

'Yeah, not bad,' his mother added. Mark closed his eyes and smiled, feeling the breeze on his face. He was very happy to be there with his parents. It seemed so long since they had last done something together as a family. They were quite lucky with the weather, too: the sky was clear and it was warm. Mark's face was sweaty after the climb.

'Let's take a break,' his mother suggested. 'We could sit over there.' She pointed at a patch of grass between two expanses of low blueberry bushes.

'Yes, let's stop for lunch,' his father agreed. 'Later we can go to the hill next to this one – there's a viewpoint there that looks like the ruins of an old fortress. They say that on a fine day like today you can see ten counties from that hill. You're going to like it, Mark.'

'I'm sure I am,' Mark said, eagerly.

The Lickey Hills Park was yet another place in Birmingham he hadn't explored yet. He used to wander around the city alone, taking buses at random, just to see where they would take him. But now he thought it would be nice to come here with Tandi one day and climb the same hills, pick blueberries until their hands turned purple from the juice and look at the ten counties from the viewpoint.

'I used to come here quite often when I was your age,' Mark's father said.

'Yes, your father and I came here on a couple of dates,' his mother added. Mark thought it strange that his mother mentioned dates. He hadn't told his parents about Tandi yet. He didn't know how to approach the subject, or how to bring her into the conversation. And he found it hard to reveal something that had become quite personal in the last few weeks. He knew that Tandi considered him a friend and he considered her a friend too, but did she feel something more for him?

He just felt confused about everything. Far too many events had happened in the past few months: his father drinking, that row between his parents after which he left and met Tandi, talking to her about everything, teaching her how to carve, his parents making up, his father not drinking anymore, the three of them finally finding time to go somewhere as a family… and, most confusingly of all, the horses he kept seeing. He had hoped that once his father had stopped drinking, he wouldn't see them anymore, but since that time in the forest with Tandi, he had seen them twice more. Both times, it was only a brief glimpse, and then they disappeared. Mark really didn't know what to make of it. When it came to his feelings towards Tandi, Mark knew deep down exactly how he felt (although he didn't want to admit it, even to himself). Yet, when he tried to figure out what those revolting horses meant and why he kept seeing them, his head was empty.

Trying to look busy, Mark took the picnic blanket out of his backpack and spread it on the ground. His father took his own bag off his shoulder and produced several plastic boxes with food: sandwiches, cold cuts of meat and sliced vegetables. Mark's mother opened a bottle of home-made juice.

'Hey, Mark, do you still go exploring around the city?' his father asked. 'I know you liked that in the past.'

'I still like that,' Mark said. 'And I still do. There are all sorts of amazing things in the most ordinary places.'

'And you won't find a more ordinary place than Birmingham, I can tell you that,' his father said, laughing.

'Oh, come on, Dad!' Mark said. 'Recently I went to Moseley with a friend and she showed me this amazing spot. It's as if you're, like, in a forest in the middle of the city! You can't even hear the traffic from the roads, you know.'

'She?' his father asked. 'You've got a female friend?'

Damn it! That wasn't the way he'd wanted the conversation to go.

'We're just friends,' Mark said, simply. 'She likes exploring things too. I used to do it alone, but it's nice when someone shows you a side of the city you've missed.'

'What's her name?' his mother asked.

'Tandi. Tandi Bryce,' Mark said.

'That's an unusual name,' his father said.

'Yeah, she's Jamaican.'

'Mark, your dad and I have news for you,' his mother said suddenly. 'It looks like you're going to be a big brother.'

Mark's hand with a sandwich in it stopped in mid-air. He was happy that his parents had changed the topic and didn't ask any more questions about his 'female friend', but this was an unexpected turn of events to say the least.

'Really?' he said. 'Mum, are you having a baby?'

'Yes, really,' his mother replied. Mark caught himself smiling. An only child, he had sometimes thought about the idea of having a little brother or sister and even asked his parents for one when he was little, but somehow it never came to pass. Now, when he thought about it, he was really enthusiastic about the news.

'I can see that you're happy to hear it,' his father observed.

'Very happy,' Mark said. He was. 'It's rather unexpected, though. You sure?' he asked his mother. 'It's not a joke?'

She burst into laughter.

'What?' he asked.

'You're just like your father,' she replied, laughing. 'He asked exactly the same question when I told him I was going to have you!'

'I didn't!' his father burst out.

'Yes, you did!' his mother said, laughing even more. Mark laughed with them. For the first time in many months, he felt relaxed. He thought about the news. He was going to be a big brother! He wasn't prepared for that, but he already liked the idea.

Chapter 19

Mark

Mark and Tandi reached Kings Norton Junction Bridge, where they usually parted. The bridge was ancient: its bricks looked worn, the angles of the bricks had become round and the steps that led onto it also looked as if many feet had trodden over them. Mark remembered that the stairs were rather slippery when it was raining or snowing.

The bridge arched its back over the dark waters where the Birmingham and Worcester canal joined the Stratford-on-Avon canal. Mark knew there were two spots on the canal where the water was rather wide and deep: there, under the bridge and in another place, not too far from his home. In both places, there was also a drop of a few yards from the edge of the bank to the surface of the water.

'Alright,' Mark said, after a deep breath. 'This bridge is the last stop.'

Today he did something that he hadn't thought he'd ever do: he organised a treasure hunt for Tandi. He'd written a number of clues on small cards and hidden them in different places around Kings Norton and Bourneville, with one clue leading to another. They had been hunting for them all afternoon and evening and now, as the sun was setting and the gathering clouds were making the sky darker than it usually was, Mark was ready to reveal the last one.

'I've got the last clue in my bag,' he said. He put his hand inside his bag, fished out a white card and gave it to Tandi. She read the last clue, scrawled in Mark's uneven handwriting:

'What's black, mucky and covered in thistle,
And can be called using a whistle?'

'Well, that's easy,' she said. 'It must be Spot!'

Mark knew that this one wouldn't be hard: he was sure Tandi remembered how they had first met. Besides, the answer was standing right at their feet, wagging his tail.

'Except it wasn't thistle, it was burdock,' she pointed out. 'And it wasn't covered, it was just a few small pieces.'

'There's no rhyme for *burdock*,' Mark said with a shrug. He was pleased: the treasure hunt had gone well, Tandi really enjoyed it (this made him especially happy) and they'd covered about ten miles, walking and running. Mark started to take an active part in walking Tandi's dog: it was good for both of them. Labradors need exercise, Tandi had told him, otherwise can they grow fat very quickly. Mark volunteered to walk Spot and run with him because he wanted some exercise too, in addition to his school football training.

'That's right,' Mark said, unzipping his backpack and pulling out the carved figurine of the black Labrador Retriever he had made the day after he'd met Tandi.

'That's your prize,' he said, smiling nervously and feeling slightly embarrassed. Oh, come on, why is he blushing!

Tandi took the painted carving and looked at it, and her eyes widened.

'It's the spitting image!' she said as a surprised smile lit up her face. 'When did you make it?'

'Well, a while ago,' Mark said casually. 'Glad you like it.'

Mark looked at Tandi, into her eyes. She wanted to say something, but suddenly her attempt was interrupted by loud quacking. A couple of ducks emerged from under the bridge and paddled away, seemingly unaware of the two people and a dog standing above them. Tandi looked down at the ducks and laughed.

'What is it?' Mark asked.

'Gosh, they're loud!' Tandi said. 'I can have a pretty loud voice when I want to – usually I use it to call Spot – but these guys could beat me hands down.'

'Oh, I think you could be louder than those two,' he said, laughing.

Tandi give him a look of mock indignation.

'You talk like I'm screaming all the time!' she said. 'But actually, once my voice also saved me. I was small back then, only five or so. My dad and I were walking in Sutton Park and I got lost. I was running somewhere, not watching my way, the way kids usually do, you know. So I emerged in some sort of a clearing with nobody around. I was chasing some ducks down the brook, so it took a while before I realised I got lost. Dad had met some friends and stopped to talk, and he told me not to wander too far away. I never had until that time, you know, but there's a first time for everything.

'When I realised I'd got lost, I got so scared! All the trees looked the same and I couldn't see where I'd come from. So I started calling my dad. And it was he who heard me first. I didn't hear him calling me until he was quite close. It's funny, I remember what I was thinking about when I went chasing after those ducks. I wondered how come their feet don't get cold because they're swimming in the water all year round.'

'Dunno,' Mark said, 'I never thought about it. But they're quite plump, so perhaps that keeps them warm.

I've heard of puppy fat, so maybe there is also ducky fat?'

Tandi giggled. Mark looked into her eyes again and his thoughts started racing. His heart began hammering against his ribcage so loudly that he was sure the entire street could hear it. His knees were shivering. The evening was quite cool for July, and he put his hands in his pockets to warm them up.

It was now or never. He had to do it.

He took a deep breath and took Tandi's hand into his. It felt so warm against his palm.

'I like spending time with you,' he said. For a second, he panicked: what if she pulled her hand out of his grip? But she didn't.

'I like spending time with you, too.'

Mark took a step closer to Tandi and leant slightly forward. She leant closer to him. Mark felt like he was having a fever. He tilted his head and their noses brushed past one another. Their lips touched; Mark felt as if a jolt of electricity had surged through him. The church bell sounded somewhere in the distance, blending with the faint noise of the evening traffic and then all the sounds faded, overpowered by the pounding of blood in his ears. Tandi's lips were so hot! Slowly, he pulled away and looked at her. She was smiling nervously, probably just like he was.

'Well, well, well! Isn't this just fucking cute!'

Mark felt as if icy water had filled his lungs. His palms were slippery with sweat, but this had nothing to do with the kiss. He looked around, startled. He knew that voice – a cold, piercing voice that made his hair stand on end. He looked into the distance and then he saw them at the end of the canal towpath, moving in their direction. Two pale figures in white overalls. Two horse heads. Two pairs of eyes, darker than the descending night.

They were still very far away, but Mark heard them as if they were standing right next to him.

'You just fucking look at them, all lovey-dovey,' the horse figure on the left said. 'Rahab, I think the lover boy piece of shit has found himself a bitch.' The voice was high-pitched, like a woman's, but Mark could not imagine any woman having such a voice: her tone was like the howling of the winter wind, devoid of any life or hope. If the feeling of being lonely in the dark could be expressed in sounds, this was what it would sound like.

'How about we get both of them, then?' the other horse said.

'Yeah, get rid of him, and the bitch will make a nice toy, don't you think?'

The figures were approaching them with incredible speed. They'd already gone half of the distance towards the bridge. Spot must have sensed something:

he looked in the direction of the horse figures and growled.

'What is it, Spot?' Tandi asked, anxiously looking in the same direction. Mark knew it would sound ridiculously stupid, but he had no choice.

'Tandi,' he whispered. 'You need to get out of here. Now!'

'What is it, Mark?' she said, looking down the towpath. And then suddenly her eyes widened. Mark saw fear in her face.

'There's no time to explain,' he whispered. 'Run!'

To his surprise, the usually stubborn Tandi spun on her heels.

'Spot, run!' she said quietly and clearly.

The creatures saw it. There were still about twenty yards between them and the bridge when both of them suddenly charged and jumped into the air. Mark saw them approach as the slimy extensions at the ends of their forelimbs turned into claws and their gaping jaws opened, revealing blackened mouths.

Somehow he knew they were after Tandi first, not him. Mark did not hesitate for a second: the simmering rage at these beings for following him at every step of his life boiled over. As soon as he saw where the horses were going to land, he flung himself forwards, his foot flew in the air to collide with one of the horses' abdomens and his fist flew out, ready to meet its masked face.

Yet, the collision did not happen. Instead, Mark felt as if he'd been trapped in a room full of stinking, choking smoke for several long seconds. He couldn't breathe in or out and his hands felt cold and clammy now.

Then the creature dissolved and he landed on the pavement with a thud. Pain shot through his shoulder as Mark slid about four feet down the pavement and then rolled over a few times before stopping. He lifted his head, searching for Tandi and saw her disappearing round the corner at the end of the street. Still, somehow he'd managed to stop the horses, too: he saw them stumble as they were getting up from the pavement.

One of the horses stepped towards Mark, leant over him and hoisted him up by the collar. Its white overalls stood out in the dim light that reached them from the nearby streets. The horse's mask looked sickly-pallid in the surrounding darkness. But no night could ever match the blackness of its eyes. No light was reflected in them.

'You are a cheeky little shite,' it said in a growling voice. 'Never mind your little bitch. We can do what we've come to do without her.'

Mark shook his head, trying to concentrate. The pain in his shoulder pulsated more and more intensely, and his hands smarted and were bleeding as he had scraped the skin off his palms trying to break his fall.

The horse's breath reeked of drink. Mark closed his eyes, feeling weaker with each word the creature was saying.

The horse's hideous limbs closed around his neck. Its fingers – or whatever it had where horses usually have hooves – felt like cold, slimy driftweed. Then its knee shot upwards as it kicked him in the stomach. Mark felt he was going to throw up. The world went dark. He felt a pull at his jacket as the creature yanked him upwards and pushed him over the side of the bridge and into the canal.

Chapter 20

George

George had spent all day assembling the scaffolding for the new hostel they were building for workers on oil rigs in Scotland. He returned to his own hostel, picked up a newspaper, turned on the TV to create some background noise and started reading, without any particular interest. It had been an unusually hot day for Scotland – he felt a slight prickling at the back of his neck and on his arms, which, to his surprise, had been tanned pink.

He was back in Scotland again, not too far from where his stepfather grew up. He should visit the old village in the next couple of days, he thought. They used to go there quite a lot when he was little. He should visit the old churchyard. His stepfather still had a brother in the village, George's uncle. Yes, he should definitely go there. But not today: he was a little too tired.

The news on TV was boring and George felt rather tired and sleepy. The letters in the paper started floating and shimmering before his eyes…

'Alone again, Georgie Porgie, are you?'

George jumped on the sofa. He had begun to doze off but the voice woke him with a start. He turned towards Rahab who was standing in the corner.

'Sorry, I'm not in the mood,' George grunted.

'I don't mean to twist your words, but what are these *mood swings*? You know what they say, George: if a person is annoyed by small things, it means something big is not working out. What is bothering you, George? What is eating you? You can tell me anything – I know you inside out.'

'If you know me inside out, then you should know that sometimes I want to be left alone. Like now.'

'Alone,' Rahab repeated, saying it slowly, as if savouring every letter of the word. 'We're back to where we started. You say *sometimes* you want to be left alone, but alone is what you've been for most of your life.'

'What do you mean?' George asked softly. 'I've not been alone. I had my parents, my stepfather. I have my wife, my son, my mates…'

'I think we have explored the topic of your parents in enough depth to understand that you were not very close to your father. As for your stepfather… you realised that you wanted to talk to him about many things when it was too late. And your mother, George – what have you ever spoken about? How your day was. Or what the surface of your life looked like! What about your most secret desires? Your deepest fears and the nightmares about your father? Your feelings towards women or your sexual fantasies?'

'I can't believe what I'm hearing!' George exclaimed. 'It's only polite not to tell your own mother about some of those things – it saves her a massive headache!'

'Your poor mother, George. She departed early, too, long before your stepfather: all those times your father abused you and her, none of this passes without a trace. There were scars on her body and her soul. Many many tiny wounds... thanks to your father, she passed long before her time.'

George was silent. He sensed that Rahab was feeling sad about something.

'And politeness, Georgie... politeness is just another name for being afraid,' Rahab said dryly. 'But it's okay to be afraid sometimes. To be afraid to tell some things to the people whom you do not completely trust.'

'I am quite certain about how I feel about my family, thank you very much, and...'

'I know how you feel about them, too,' Rahab said, cutting George off. 'For example, I know you loved your sister very much and she loved you too. She shared so many of her secrets with you. But what have you ever shared with her?'

George fell silent at this accusation, trying to remember at least one thing he had told his sister and no one else, but failing.

'And all this time, even if I was with you, you were alone. I was there for you, but you never felt my presence. But not to worry, George – I am used to people pushing me away even after they have known me. I am *the stone which the builders rejected.*'

A few seconds of silence followed. Memories swept over George. He was in church with his stepfather. There were candles all around, and the priest was reading the sermon with these words in it: *The stone which the builders rejected has become the head stone of the corner.* Now he was one of the builders who had rejected the Cornerstone. George stood up and looked up at Rahab who had taken off his horse mask; the familiar bearded face framed with long hair was now looking at him, with just a hint of a wise, tired smile. His eyes had no whites: they were all black, like the sky at night. So mysterious... George shuddered as if someone had splashed a bucket of icy water over him.

'I have not seen you. I have not felt your presence,' George said, lowering his head and rubbing his face. 'I feel it now. Can we put this behind us? Can we be friends? I am afraid of being alone.'

'George, this is all behind us now. Remember that I have shared my table with those whom everyone rejected. We are friends, Georgie Porgie. All you need to do is follow me.'

George nodded, but he couldn't help shuddering: it seemed that Rahab's eyes were boring right through him. They were so dark and deep… they did not reflect any light.

'And your mates, George?' Rahab continued. 'How many of them know of my existence? Why, you haven't even told your wife! Tell me, George, does your wife know about me?'

'No,' George mouthed. 'She doesn't.'

'What about your son?'

'No.'

'Good. Keep it that way. By the way, Georgie, where is your wife?'

'At home. Maybe with a friend,' George answered. 'She told me she was going to meet Mark's teacher.'

'I've asked this before, and I will ask you again, George. How sure are you of this? You don't trust her enough to tell her about your private experiences. And it's not as if the connection between me and you is something to be ashamed of. But she's a bit different from you, isn't she? She trusts you and tells you things – or so it seems. But maybe there's something she's hiding as well. Something more shameful. Something more personal – or should I say *intimate*?'

George felt his palms starting to sweat. His heart started beating faster and, to his embarrassment, he felt a dull ache in the lower part of his abdomen; he was getting aroused. George tried to hide it by sinking back into the armchair. This was strange. Why was this happening? He tried to breathe normally, but the crazy pace of his heart made this difficult. His breath was coming out in ragged rasps.

'Also, she's been staying at work longer. Why is that?'

'She got more work at the office,' George said. 'Why not?'

'Couldn't she have refused it? Or is she trying to say you're not earning enough? Or maybe she needs more money to buy herself some nice things? Who is she trying to impress? Certainly not you, George! You two are kind of past the impressing stage. Maybe she's not happy at home? Not happy in bed?'

George could not concentrate on anything. The pressure at the bottom of his stomach became unbearable. He was getting angry at the embarrassing erection and at Sarah who – *Rahab was right!* – had started spending much more time away from home. After he had started making an effort to help her more around the house and cut down on drinking!

'It only takes one handsome twenty-something, a newcomer, and one frustrated woman who is not very happy at home. You know what can happen, George.

A passing glance, a joke at lunchtime, a common topic of conversation... the results are always the same. She will give herself to him before you know it.'

'She's loyal to me! She trusts me!' George said, almost desperately.

'They call me the Knower of Hearts,' Rahab said. 'I know what is deep inside every heart — even those who do not deserve to speak to me. Who will never speak to me. Those who will kiss my feet and those who will spit in my face. I know your heart, as well as your son's and your wife's.'

'Can you tell me?' George said with hope in his voice. But he knew the answer before it came.

'No, I'm afraid I can't. It would not be fair on others. But from time to time, I am prepared to tell you some things to warn you about the dangers that might come.

'Your wife is still loyal to you,' Rahab continued. 'At least her body is entirely yours. But the danger is there, in her mind. This is where damnation is born — always in the mind. It's hidden, but inevitable.'

George winced. With every word Rahab said, the pressure in his abdomen increased and turned into a burning pain.

'What do you mean?' he asked.

'She is pregnant, George. Anything can happen now between her and this... rival I told you about, and no one will notice. No consequences. Be alert, George. Be careful.'

Rahab stepped in front of George.

'I see that something is embarrassing you,' he said. 'But there's nothing to be embarrassed about.'

George felt as if something cold had entered his lungs. Rahab's voice had changed: it was a woman's voice now. Warm, powerful and seductive.

The horse put on its mask and stepped into the large mirror on the wall. Once inside the mirror, it removed the mask again, and George thought he had begun to lose his mind. Under the mask, there was a woman. She had olive-coloured skin and hair the colour of burning coal – black with stripes of fiery red. It was Lilith, the same woman he had glimpsed in the shower the other day. Without saying a word, she slipped off her white robe. Underneath it, she was naked.

'Do not fear me,' she said, sliding through the glass, coming towards him and pressing her full breasts against his arm. 'I am yet another face of the One you already know.'

George watched, as if from outside his own body, as the woman unbuttoned his shirt and unbuckled his belt.

'Let me help you get rid of your embarrassment,' she said, slipping her hand inside his trousers. 'For there is nothing to be embarrassed about. There is strength in both your arms and your loins.'

The room spun around George. Pleasure swelled inside him and spread like ink spreads in water, in ornate twirling plumes. Smoke and steam covered everything and the woman took George as he lost control entirely.

Chapter 21

Mark

Mark went down with a splash before he could understand what was going on. Water surrounded him and he felt weightless. There was something strange about the canal. It felt as if there was a current which was dragging him deeper. Mark emerged, spluttering and coughing, spitting out the water.

He shook his head and looked up at the bridge. What he saw made icy emptiness fill his stomach. Suddenly, all of the horse figures' features began transforming. They lost everything that was human-like about them: their postures changed until they turned into ugly hunchbacks; their limbs stretched and twisted out of shape, becoming long, bent needles that aimed to pierce the sky. The whiteness of their hides stood out against the darkness that had fallen so suddenly, and it hurt Mark's eyes to look at them.

And then they jerked their heads towards the sky and started whinnying and groaning in a rhythmic cacophony as if shouting out some sinister incantation.

Mark felt the water around him ripple and then bubble. Something strange was definitely happening to the usually peaceful waters of the canal: currents began circling around him, becoming stronger and stronger each second. Suddenly, all light disappeared from the world, and only the horses' hides blazed before him. They and the movements in the water of the canal were the only things he could see.

Suddenly, a strong undercurrent blasted him towards the wall of the canal. He thrust his arms out to avoid colliding with the bricks covered in slimy seaweed. His arms took the impact as the current spun his body sideways and then backed away. He could clearly see the current as it moved away from him and started circling rapidly a couple of yards away. The shrill neighing of the horse figures echoed in his ears, making his eardrums vibrate. Somewhere through this, he heard a rumbling of thunder that became louder with every second. The current circled faster and faster, drawing other currents towards itself, and then, with a sudden sucking and slurping sound, a vortex opened up on the surface of the water, growing into a whirlpool that sucked Mark towards itself.

Mark was not a bad swimmer – he went to the local council pool regularly – but he had never been drawn away by strong currents anywhere and didn't know what to do in a whirlpool. The water spun him around and he lost all sense of direction. He felt he was also losing his strength and wouldn't be able to hold on for much longer.

Mark's breath came in short, painful gasps. The water was taking his energy away. The thunder was now as loud as the hysterical neighing of the horses and the beating of his heart that thumped in his ears like a bass drum. Suddenly, another current rushed past his lower body, dragging him under the water, into the centre of the whirlpool.

All sound and light disappeared. Mark could only feel the stinging cold water coming up his nose, and an overwhelming sense of panic. *I must resurface,* he thought frantically. Something inside of him, almost subconsciously, told him to dive deeper and dart to the side. He did so and thrashed his arms and kicked his legs like mad until he felt his muscles were about to explode with pain, but finally he managed to re-emerge from the water. He almost screamed as he breathed in and out.

Then he felt another current. The whirlpool that had stopped for a second or two started spinning again and moved towards him. His strength was running out and he would not make it a second time.

And then everything stopped. The waters of the canal moved no more. The usual streetlights, although few and far between, were back. And there was another figure dressed in white running towards the canal. Mark would have recognised this man anywhere. It was Oak.

The old man gathered his white robes, then grasped at an old rusty iron bar that was hanging over the canal and jumped down. He rammed the soles of his shoes into the wall, securing his position and extended his free hand towards Mark.

'Come on, laddie!' he shouted. 'Grab hold of me!'

Mark managed to grasp the man's huge, fleshy palm just when he felt he could not keep swimming any more. To his surprise, he didn't need to do anything else. Oak's fingers locked around Mark's wrist and the old man started pulling himself upwards with Mark hanging onto him. The next thing Mark knew, he was out of the water.

'Grab my shoulder with your other hand!' Oak commanded. Mark did as he was told and then Oak heaved both of them onto the stony bank as if Mark did not weigh anything at all.

Bloody hell, he's as strong as a bear! he thought.

'Y'awright, laddie?' the old man boomed. Mark opened his mouth but could not speak at all, so he just nodded. He was trembling all over with cold and exhaustion.

'You look a right mess here, young man,' Oak said, looking at Mark's face. 'Lucky I was passing by. How did you manage to fall in?'

Mark didn't quite know how to answer this. Mad as Oak was, the truth would sound even madder.

He thought about Tandi. How was she? Had she managed to get home all right? He had to get home as soon as possible and call her. Mark pushed himself up and they started walking.

'Try to move as fast as you can,' Oak said. 'We need to get you home as soon as possible. So, how did you fall in?'

'Someone... pushed me in,' Mark gasped, breathing heavily. Walking fast hurt. His shoulder felt as if someone had hit it with a hammer.

At this moment, something happened to Oak's face. The usually calm and even somewhat otherworldly features, the expression that people usually called 'being in a world of your own', were distorted by a grimace of disgust.

'Fucking bastards!' he said through gritted teeth. 'Did you see which way they went?' he asked, looking Mark straight in the face. The boy recoiled at the old man's expression. He had never seen him this angry.

'No, sir, I didn't,' Mark said. 'Something happened... I went underwater...'

He remembered the currents and the sucking slurping whirlpool. How on earth was he going to explain to anyone what had just happened? He needed to invent a good story to tell at home – they were almost there.

'Is that where you live, laddie?' Oak asked, pointing at his front door. Mark nodded, looking back at him – the old man had calmed down and his bearded face was now filled with concern. Just as he was frantically thinking of the best possible lie to explain his soaked mucky clothes, Oak took the handle of the brass knocker and knocked on the door of Mark's house.

His mother opened the door. She looked down at Mark and gasped.

'My god, Mark, what happened?' she asked, pressing her hand to her mouth. 'There isn't a dry thread on you. Come in, quickly, and get changed!' Sarah opened the door wide, letting him in.

Before Mark could say anything, Oak started speaking:

'Your son was attacked,' he said. 'He put up a good fight but was pushed into the canal.'

'Attacked?' Sarah asked, her eyes widening in horror. 'What happened?'

'There were two of them,' Mark said. 'They pushed me into the water.'

'Were you on your own?' Mark's mother asked.

'No, I... I was with a friend,' he said after a short hesitation. 'I was with Tandi.'

'Is she okay?' Sarah asked with concern.

'She... she ran away,' Mark said. 'I fought them on my own. I need to phone her.'

Mark rushed back into the hall where the landline phone was hanging on the wall. He lifted the receiver and punched in Tandi's number.

Eight excruciating double bleeps later, Tandi picked up the phone.

'Hello?'

The voice on the other end was tired and strained, and all of a sudden, Mark felt lost for words. What would he tell her? Had she seen any of the fight? To her, it must have looked like he was chasing ghosts. What would she say? How could he explain why he had asked her to run away?

'Tandi,' he exhaled.

'Mark!'

It sounded like she was glad to hear him. Relief washed over him: he was afraid she'd hang up as soon as she heard his voice. 'Mark, are you okay?'

'Yeah, I... I guess I'm fine.'

'Are you hurt?'

'No, no, I'm fine, really.' Wait! Why was she asking this? He felt confused.

'Tandi,' he said after a pause. 'About what just happened... We have to talk.'

'Yes, we have to. As soon as possible, but not on the phone. Mark, I know you had a fight. What happened?'

Mark fell silent as the message hit home.

'I fell into the canal,' he said, finally. 'I was pulled out by my neighbour, Oak. Remember him?'

'I do,' she said. 'He's creepy.'

'He saved my life. And he's not creepy, just strange and harmless.'

Mark's thoughts were racing. Somehow he felt that, at the other end of the line, Tandi was eager to say something but was bracing herself before she could muster the courage to say it out loud. And then she did, lowering her voice to a whisper:

'Mark, I know who you fought today.'

'Sorry?'

'I can see them too.'

Mark fell silent for a couple of seconds.

'What?' he finally said, dumbstruck. 'How come...'

'I can't say any more than that. Not on the phone. We have to talk as soon as possible. Meet me tomorrow if you can.'

'Alright. Our bench. Where we first met. You free in the morning?'

'Yes. Is 10 o'clock okay?'

'Yes, that's fine. See you then.'

And then she hung up. Mark returned to the kitchen where his mother and Oak were sitting.

'Your son's a brave lad,' Oak said.

'If you weren't around, sir, I would have drowned,' Mark said. 'Oak pulled me out,' he explained to his mother.

Tears sparkled in Sarah's eyes. She threw her arms around both Mark and Oak, hugging them tightly. The old man seemed to be slightly embarrassed by this.

'It's okay, madam,' he said. 'Just lucky I was around, that's all. I know how hard it is to swim with soaking clothes on.'

'Come on, sit down, both of you,' Sarah said, wiping her eyes with the edge of her apron. 'I'll make you some tea. And Mark,' she added suddenly, looking at him, 'why haven't you changed yet? Come on, before you catch pneumonia!'

Mark rushed upstairs to his room, pulled off all of his sodden clothes and dumped them into a plastic bag. Next, he took a towel from a drawer and dried himself hastily. There would be time to take a shower later.

Mark changed into dry clothes and rushed out of his room. As he walked downstairs, back into the kitchen, his thoughts were racing. He couldn't believe what Tandi had told him. *Mark, I know who you fought today. I can see them too.* This certainly came as a shock.

What did all this mean? Did that mean she had heard what they said as well? He felt rather proud, though – after all, it was he who had saved her. They wanted to harm her, but he hadn't let them. He had fended them off. *He had fought for her!*

He walked into the kitchen and took a mug of tea from the tabletop.

'Mark,' his mother said. 'Are you okay?'

'Mum, I'm fine,' Mark said. 'I just… got wet.'

'Did you see who attacked you? Their faces?'

'No, I didn't,' Mark replied. 'It was so quick. I just told Tandi to run and they jumped onto me and threw me into the water.'

'Is your friend alright?'

'She's fine. She got home safely. I'll meet her tomorrow, just to make sure she's okay.'

'What about the attackers? Should we tell the police?'

Mark hadn't thought of this possibility. What would he tell the police? Would they show him mug-shots of criminals and ask him if he recognised any? Was he prepared for that? He didn't think so.

'I don't know,' he said. 'But since I didn't know them and didn't see them too well and nothing happened, really… perhaps we should just forget about it.'

'I don't like the idea of forgetting about it, but maybe you're right,' his mother said. 'I just don't see why someone would attack you.'

'Perhaps they were just drunk,' Oak suggested.

'Perhaps,' Sarah agreed.

*

Oak left their house as soon as he had finished the cup of tea that Mark's mother had given him. Mark was so tired he fell asleep immediately, as soon as his head touched the pillow. His last thoughts before he fell asleep were about Tandi.

Mark's dreams that night were troubled. First he saw a dark room full of shelves and drawers and a tall, skinny man dressed in a pearly-grey cloak who was rummaging through them, throwing their contents on the ground, looking for something and not being able to find it. The cloak, which emitted faint, ghostly light, concealed the man's face and body, but Mark could see that the man was disfigured. He was limping and his back was bent at an unnatural angle, as if had been broken. For some reason, it seemed to Mark that the man had fallen from an incredible height. The man was getting angrier and angrier, hammering his fists on the old shelves until the wood snapped like dry bones. Wood chips flew in all directions and objects crashed onto the floor.

Suddenly a door creaked and the room was flooded with more faint, ghostly light. The man's pearly cloak changed colour, becoming darker.

The view changed. Two horse figures were kneeling before a jagged black figure that stood facing them. Mark could see only its silhouette.

'Fools! Idiots!' the shadowy figure shrieked. Then it backhanded the first horse across the face. There was a slap on the flesh and the wet crunch of a bone breaking. With a sharp intake of breath, the horse went down on the floor, covering its head with its forelimbs. Another punch, another wet crunch and the other horse was down as well. The shadow lifted something like a black club or mace and blows rained on both horses, cracking bones underneath their hides with disgusting wet snapping and slurping sounds.

The horses took the punishment with a meekness he had never seen before. Each time they had appeared before Mark, they had stood proud and arrogant, watching the scene as if it were a play they were directing. But now it looked as if the shadowy figure, whatever it was, held immense power over them.

'Never! Did you hear that? Never! Take the matters! Into your own hands!' the figure screamed. 'The boy dies when I say he dies!'

The hand wielding the mace never stopped. The mace rose and fell mercilessly. The horses neither neighed nor screamed; they only hissed and snarled in pain as blood pooled under their pearly-white hides, oozing through the ruptured skin where the club hit them. The blood was black as oil or shoe polish. Mark felt a sudden wave of nausea rush over him.

The picture changed again. All of the colours blurred into a dark spinning whirlpool, and then a bloodied mouth with broken teeth appeared in the centre of it and sang in a howling voice, like a cackling jackal:

Georgie Porgie pudding and pie,
Your daddy made your mummy cry.
Your daddy's bound to rot in hell,
But you'll be joining him as well!

The nausea became unbearable. Mark woke up, ran to the toilet and retched until he felt empty and his stomach could heave out nothing more. Finally, he lowered himself onto the floor to catch his breath.

Chapter 22

Sarah

Sarah was woken up by footsteps in the hall on the first floor and then in the kitchen. She glanced at the electronic alarm clock on the bedside table. Half past two in the morning. She heard the clumsy slapping of bare feet on the wooden flooring and realised that it was Mark making those noises. What happened? Why was he up so late? Had he slept at all?

She didn't know why she couldn't get rid of the feeling that something strange had happened that night. She didn't know what it was, but the gut feeling all mothers have told her that there was more to it than just a fight. She had a lot of questions for Mark, but he had gone to bed before she had a chance to ask him anything. She noticed that his clothes smelt funny. It was not just the smell of dirty water; there was another smell that gave her the shivers: dead, rotting plants. There was something... otherworldly in that smell. Something that made her want to run away as far as possible. She had put all the clothing in the washing machine and poured in double the usual amount of washing powder.

Since her son wasn't sleeping, it was a good time to talk to him. It had been a while since they had talked properly. Sarah stretched in the bed that was too big for her now that George had gone on a business trip to Scotland. They were building a new hotel to the north of Edinburgh. Sarah knew that George's stepfather Chris McRae was born near Edinburgh. Perhaps going to the places where he used to spend his childhood summers would do her husband some good.

Sarah slipped her nightgown on and went down into the kitchen. Mark was taking the kettle off the hob and pouring water into a mug.

'What's the matter, Mark, dear?' Sarah asked. 'Can't sleep?'

Mark spun on his heels, looking slightly startled.

'Oh, it's you, Mum,' he said. 'Sorry, am I too loud?'

'No, no, sweetie,' Sarah said, 'I can't sleep, just like you.' She sniffed the air and sensed the sour smell of bile.

'Are you feeling okay?' she asked, worried. 'Have you been sick?'

'I have,' he answered, looking somewhat embarrassed. 'Must have swallowed some water from the canal.'

Sarah went towards her son and pressed her lips to his forehead, feeling his temperature. His skin felt cold and sweaty.

'Come on, Mum, I'm okay,' Mark protested. Sarah smiled to herself, despite her worries: her son was behaving like a normal teenage boy and didn't want her to get all touchy-feely with him. Mark went towards the kitchen table and made tea in two mugs: one with honey for himself and one with milk for her. Sarah took her mug and nodded appreciatively.

'Thank you, son,' she whispered. 'You're a big lad now – I haven't even noticed how you've grown.'

She smiled as she saw Mark blush in response to her words: he was always so humble about things.

'Come on, Mum, it's just a cup of tea,' he said.

'It's the fact that you made two,' she said, smiling. 'You know how to take care of other people. That's a good trait to have. Girls like it.'

She watched Mark sip his hot tea, trying to hide his blushing face behind the huge mug. But he was smiling as well, apparently pleased with her compliments. For a while, they slowly drank their tea in silence and she watched Mark hold the mug with both hands and inhale the scent of linden flower honey. Then he said:

'Mum, I'm worried about Dad.'

'Why?' Sarah asked. 'He's doing much better than before, you know he is. He's not drinking. We've been out together. What's wrong?'

Yet, Sarah was worried about George herself. She was glad that things were improving; George had given her and Mark a lot of attention but there was something, some bitter aftertaste that made her anxious about her husband's state. George had been very quiet and secretive recently, and she didn't like it. The

George she knew was not quiet, definitely not reticent – not with her, at least. She didn't like the feeling but couldn't shake it off. Her husband was hiding something.

'Dunno, Mum,' Mark whispered. 'Perhaps I'm just worried that he might drink again.'

'He won't,' Sarah said firmly. She still believed that as long as she thought about good things, bad things wouldn't happen. 'He's better than before. Much better.

'I'm sorry you've had to hear us arguing,' she added. It must have been nasty. Me shouting at your father all the time.'

'The entire situation was nasty,' Mark said. 'You were only doing what you thought was right.'

Her son saw her point of view and Sarah was glad about it, but she still felt ashamed of venting her anger for the entire neighbourhood to hear.

'What happened to Aunt Celia must have hit him hard,' Mark added after a brief pause. 'He's not been taking it too well.'

'It's been improving. He's better now,' Sarah repeated and sipped her tea. She lowered her voice to a whisper even though there was no need to as George was not there.

'Your father wouldn't want you to hear any of this,' she said. 'He's a very proud man and just can't admit he's got a weakness. His weakness – in his view – isn't the drinking. Your father's tough, all right – once, when we'd just started dating, we were walking at night and three drunken thugs attacked us. He fought them off single-handedly.'

She and George had made love for the first time that night. Sarah's thoughts went back to that time. She closed her eyes, savouring the memory and then opened them and blushed, embarrassed about reliving something very intimate in front of her son.

She was no saint: although she had been raised in a strict religious environment, she had had sexual relationships with two men who she thought cared about her before she met George. Still, somehow, either due to her upbringing or for another reason, it had felt wrong every time. Both relationships ended a couple of months after she'd had sex. The first man liked doing it while drunk: a can or two of beer followed by a shot of spirits. He said it helped him perform better, and he only wanted to make her feel good. After they broke up, Sarah vowed never to sleep with a drunken man again, a promise which she kept.

George was the first man with whom sex seemed the most natural thing. It just felt so right. It still felt so right.

'But on the other hand, your father is a very emotional person,' she continued, leaving her thoughts and focusing on the present again. 'And he's always seen that as a weakness. He has always tried not to show his feelings to the world. He's hidden what he feels from the people he doesn't trust.'

'He trusted you enough to show his feelings to you, though,' Mark said.

Great mums and sons think alike, Sarah thought with a smile.

'You're right, sweetie,' she said. 'If you're afraid to show your feelings, then you're afraid to love.'

George was the first man to whom she had not been afraid to truly show how she felt.

'Talking of feelings, Mark,' Sarah added, looking at her son, 'How's your girlfriend doing?'

'What?'

Mark's jaw dropped, making him open his mouth. This was really not a question he'd expected to hear, Sarah thought. He looked so funny, gawping like a fish out of water, and Sarah couldn't help but laugh.

'What's so funny, Mum?' Mark asked, slightly offended.

'Nothing... just your expression.' She tried to control her laughter. 'The friend you were with when you were attacked, Tandi. She's a girl, right? A girl and a friend equals a girlfriend, doesn't it?'

'No, it doesn't,' Mark said, defensively. 'She's not... well...' Sarah saw him blush again.

'Come on, don't be shy,' Sarah said. 'She is, right?'

After a few more seconds of awkward silence, Mark finally gave in.

'Yes.'

'And you like her.'

Mark didn't even nod. This was not a question.

'And it's her you've been seeing for the past few weeks.'

Another statement which should have been a question. Mark looked at his mother incredulously.

'Mum, honestly! How do you know?'

'Well,' Sarah said with a smile. 'We women use more than one sense to get information about the world around us. Something told me there was someone in your life – let's just call it a "mother's gut feeling". But my gut feeling was confirmed when I saw you ironing a T-shirt. Boys don't do that unless there's a special reason. And when you called her today, after you came home, I saw how worried you were. I know what that means.'

'Unbelievable!' Mark said, shaking his head.

'By the way, Tandi is also a woman and she also has the ability to see what others don't see. I can bet you she knows you like her. So, have you already told her that?'

This was prying, but it was the best chance for Sarah to talk to her son properly. He'd been almost as secretive and reclusive as his father. Mark raised his eyes from the mug, hesitated for a second and said:

'I have.'

Sarah decided to take things one step further.

'Have you kissed?'

More silence.

'Yes.'

Something quivered inside Sarah's chest. This was not fear for him, no – just the anticipation of the talk she knew she'd need to have with her son one day. She wished George was with her now, though. Perhaps it would have been easier.

'Did anything else happen?'

'We were attacked.'

'Ah. I see.'

Gosh, this was so bloody awkward! But why did it have to be? It was her son, after all! She had changed him, bathed him and wiped his bum when he was little!

Yet, it was not the same little boy she knew. Her son was growing up. He'd defended a woman, *his* woman!

'Mark,' she asked, blushing. 'Do you know how to use protection?'

Mark stared back at her. Poor lad, this was just a night of unexpected questions for him.

'Do you know how to put on a condom?' she repeated.

This time. Mark really didn't know how to answer.

'Yes, in theory,' he said finally. 'I was, like, expecting to have this conversation with Dad,' he added.

'Well, you're having it with me instead. I know that your father is a fan of "lads only" days, but if you want to know more about how to treat a woman, you have to ask a woman – at least that's the way it seems to me.'

Mark nodded with understanding in his eyes. He seemed to agree with her on this. She was glad of another little victory.

'Why are you asking me about... well... condoms?' he asked. 'I wasn't planning to...'

'Sex isn't a job interview, Mark. It doesn't happen when you plan it, on the scheduled day and hour. It just... happens. Plus, I know what boys are like. And I also know that things usually happen when you least expect them to happen.

'I remember my time at the orphanage; quite a few girls got pregnant when they were fifteen or sixteen. We didn't even have condoms available everywhere, especially not for free. And everyone – both boys and girls – were too shy to go to the pharmacy and just ask at the counter. Times were different, but people remain the same.'

'Did they not teach you... well, you know... sexual education at school?'

Sarah laughed at this question. Talk about the generation gap!

'I was raised in an orphanage by nuns,' she said. 'We were taught nothing about our own bodies, not to mention men's. The only thing we were taught is that the loss of blood during our periods won't kill us. They also hammered slogans about the dangers of sex into our heads. For some of us it worked, and for some it didn't. Each time a schoolgirl became pregnant, the nuns were furious. I was rather afraid of them, especially one called Sister Grey. She had these thick horn-rimmed glasses and a hooked nose that made her look like an angry owl. She was very strict: each time she told anyone off, she made them cry. It was bad enough when she shouted at me for a hastily made bed. I was afraid to imagine what would happen if I got into more trouble. Probably my fear kept me from going the same way some others girls went and I was able to finish school, find a job and marry your father. I still keep in touch with Sister Grey. Despite all their strictness, which I really didn't like when I was little, she raised me well and I'm grateful for that. There was another one called Sister Margaret. She was very kind, but she always became as strict as Sister Grey when it came to relationships between girls and boys.' Sarah thought about those times for a moment. Then she continued:

'You said Tandi is a girl and a friend. Is she a good friend?'

Sarah could see in Mark's face that this was a question he could answer with certainty.

'Yes,' he said, 'she is. We've got a lot in common.'

'That's good to hear,' Sarah said with a smile. 'A girlfriend or a boyfriend should first of all be a good friend.'

'Were you and Dad friends before you became a couple?' Mark asked.

'Yes, we were,' Sarah said. 'We still are. Our friendship quickly grew into something bigger, into love and marriage, but it wasn't replaced by them. The friendship remained. The reason I shouted at him was because I didn't like what his actions were doing to our friendship.'

Mark nodded, showing that he understood.

'Mum,' he said, 'I'm sorry I left that night. It was stupid and cowardly. I just... I didn't know what to do. It was selfish of me. I wanted to... to draw your attention to me. To stop arguing and look at me.'

'I'm also sorry you had to witness it,' his mother said. 'I was really scared for our friendship, mine and your dad's. When you love someone – as a friend, or as a spouse – you want what's best for them, not just to admire them. There was even a joke about it when I was younger. What's the difference between fake love and real love? Fake love says: Oh, the snow in your hair is so pretty and romantic! Real love says: You've lost your hat!'

Mark smiled and said:

'The last bit is a bit hard to believe. Or understand the logic of.'

'Just believe it,' Sarah said. 'You'll understand it later. And one more thing: try to spend more time with your dad. I know both his drinking and our arguments have upset you, but he needs friends more than ever now. Even if you'd rather spend time with Tandi.'

Mark felt a pang of conscience: Tandi had told him to do exactly the same thing.

'I'm sorry, Mum,' he said. 'I will do that.'

Chapter 23

Mark

Mark was marching resolutely through the park, towards the bench where he and Tandi had first met. He reached the bench and sat there, waiting. He'd come almost forty minutes early: sitting at home and waiting to leave on time was just not conceivable.

Thoughts were racing through his mind, making his head buzz. He'd hardly slept the night before: he just couldn't make the swarming thoughts go away, especially after the conversation he'd had with his mother. Too much had happened in the last twenty-four hours.

Almost as soon as he sat down, Mark saw Tandi walking towards the bench with the same resolve in her step, and with Spot at her heels like a loyal friend. He stood up to greet her. She ran towards him and threw her arms around him, hugging him close and almost knocking him down.

'Oh my God, Mark' she whispered. 'I was so worried.'

Mark hugged her back.

'Me too,' he said. 'I was worried sick.'

Her presence was so warm. He felt as if a huge helium balloon had expanded in his chest, making it hard to breathe. Tandi was wearing the same grey tracksuit that she had worn on the day they first met. It smelt of the same fabric softener. The familiar scent and colours made Mark feel better. It was fine. She was safe.

'I was so relieved when you called', Tandi whispered. Her voice was strangely hoarse. Mark pulled away, looking at her. There were tears in her eyes.

Mark raised his hands to wipe them away. For the first time in his life, he noticed how rough his hands were from all the carving and handling wood and tools. He turned his palm and gently brushed the tears away with the backs of his fingers. It was the first time he'd seen Tandi crying. And she was crying *for him*. He didn't know how that made him feel. He wished she didn't have to cry. But somewhere deep inside his chest, there was a little warm glowing light and it shone brighter when he saw how much she really cared about him.

'I was relieved when you picked up,' he replied.

Mark had a feeling that neither of them really wanted to broach the subject. And yet, this was the reason why they'd agreed to meet. Finally, Mark let go of Tandi, took her hand, looked her in the eyes and said:

'So, you can see them too.'

She nodded silently.

'They're hideous,' she said after a pause. 'They're scary like nothing else can be. And the worst thing is...' her voice trailed off.

'The eyes,' Mark finished for her.

'Yes,' Tandi said. 'So dark and empty... and cold.'

Tandi hugged him again, wrapping her arms around his waist, as if looking for warmth and protection. Mark shielded her with his arms.

'Since when?' she whispered into his shoulder. Mark knew what she was asking.

'Since my aunt died in a car accident and my dad started drinking,' he said. 'When he came home drunk and my parents argued, I saw it... almost all the time. Yesterday we saw two, but until then there'd been only one of them standing in the corner of the room.'

'Yes,' Tandi said, nodding. 'Standing in the corner, watching everything.' She shuddered and pressed herself closer to Mark. 'I started seeing them... since my parents died.'

'It's like... it's crazy,' Mark said after a pause, shaking his head.

'I'm afraid it's not. We can't both be crazy in exactly the same way. We can't have the same visions.'

Tandi was right. At least, this made sense.

'But why do we see them?' Mark asked.

'I don't know,' Tandi said. 'I wish I did.'

'How about going to your special place?' she suggested after a pause. 'I always feel better when I'm there.'

'Alright,' Mark agreed. They avoided the canal and took a different route, holding hands in silence as they walked. It was strange, Mark thought, but the silence didn't feel awkward. He felt that there was more than just words connecting them. For the first time in many months, Mark felt that someone understood him.

As they were approaching his abandoned factory, Mark sensed that something was wrong. Something had happened to the door, he saw it from a distance. Then, when they were about twenty yards away, he realised what it was: the door was ajar.

'What the...' Mark sprinted towards the entrance. The padlock had been broken and was lying on the threshold. Mark picked it up and looked at it: it had not been sawn off or broken with a crowbar. The chrome-plated shank was warped and had been twisted several times. The body of the padlock was mangled and full of holes: it looked as if a beast with steel fangs had chewed it up. Mark wondered who or what could have done this. Were they still inside?

Tandi came from behind. Mark turned to her, pressing his index finger to his lips.

'Let me have a look first,' he said. Then he stepped inside as silently as he could, peeking around the corner. There was no one inside. All was quiet. If it had been thieves, they had gone; if it had been tramps, they would still be there. Mark beckoned Tandi to come inside after him.

'Oh no,' she whispered, stifling a sob.

Mark looked around and froze on the spot with a curse on his lips.

Inside, there was a mess. All of the bookshelves had been toppled over, and all the books lay strewn on the floor with sheets ripped out of them. The tools had been scattered around the workshop and toolboxes had been smashed to pieces. The largest axe was wedged into the varnished lid of the piano.

Mark's fingers released their grip on the mutilated lock. It clattered to the floor. He was speechless: the place that was dearest to him, the memory of his grandfather, had been defiled.

'Who could've done it, Mark?' Tandi asked, squeezing his hand. He squeezed hers back.

'I don't know,' he said, 'but I saw him. Last night, in my dream. I saw a man dressed in black who was rummaging through some shelves, looking for something. I've only realised it now: it was here, in this place.'

'The trapdoor,' Tandi said suddenly. 'The chest. Is it safe?'

Mark rushed towards the far end of the room, pushing things out of his way. He reached the threadbare red carpet at the end of the room and lifted it. The trapdoor was not damaged; the padlock was still on it.

With trembling fingers, Mark reached for the keys hanging around his neck, unlocked the padlock and pulled on the iron ring that served as the handle. He breathed a sigh of relief: the chest was still there. Mark pulled it out and opened it. All the books handwritten and illustrated by Grandpa Chris were still there, intact.

Mark closed the chest, pushed it aside and stood up, stretching his back and looking at the mess around him.

'Whoever did it must have been looking for something,' he said. 'It looks like they didn't steal anything, but everything's out of place. It seems really crazy but it must be that person... or thing from my dream.'

'It sounds less crazy than both of us seeing the same thing that no one else can see,' Tandi said. 'But are you sure it's the same person from your dream?'

'I'm not,' Mark said. 'But it's my best guess. Why would someone break into this place anyway? There's nothing special in here. It looks like they just wanted to ransack it.'

'Maybe that's exactly what they wanted?' Tandi suggested.

'I don't know. I really don't,' Mark said.

'You sure they're gone?' she asked. Mark nodded, though he wasn't sure. There was definitely a connection between his dream and someone ransacking his place. Mark's thoughts returned to his dream. Who was the man beating the horses? Why were they beaten? Why had he seen it?

They had tried to kill him. He was sure of that. Had that man from his dream punished them because they had failed? Would they try again?

Nothing made sense. What did the tall, jagged man mean when he said, *The boy dies when I say he dies*? Another thought occurred to Mark. It looked as if when the horses had attacked them, it had been an act of free will, something that the jagged figure had not ordered. Were they punished for attacking him when they shouldn't have? Everything was confusing. He wasn't sure if he wanted to tell Tandi about that part of his dream.

'We need to clear up this mess,' Tandi said, pulling him from his thoughts.

'We do,' Mark agreed. 'That's the best we can do now. Luckily I have another padlock, a much heavier and more secure one, somewhere here among the tools – I can use it to lock the place up again.'

Within about three hours, the place was tidy again. Mark would need to make new toolboxes to replace the smashed ones; some books would need to be fixed as they had been ripped out of their covers; some shelves would need to be repaired as well. Still, on the whole, things were not that bad. The only thing that Mark felt particularly sorry about was the piano, but Tandi tried playing it again and assured him that it was still in good condition. Only the surface had been damaged.

'Oh, look,' Tandi said, pointing at the chest on the floor as they were finishing tidying up. 'We haven't put this one away yet.'

'Yeah, let's do it,' Mark said, squatting down, ready to grab the chest.

'Wait a moment,' Tandi said. 'May I... may I look at the books again? I really like your grandfather's drawings.'

'Yes, go ahead.' Mark heaved the chest onto the table. Tandi took out a leather-bound book and opened it. They sat down on the old sofa under the window. There wasn't enough light: the window was stained with dirt and Mark lit a small lamp. They sat there, leafing through the pages.

Despite the shock of the situation, Mark enjoyed the moment of closeness they shared. This girl was incredible, he thought. She understood him. She was worried about him. She liked his carvings. He liked her paintings, too. He'd never felt that way before.

Tandi gasped, interrupting his thoughts.

'Mark,' she said, pointing at the book, 'look at this.'

Mark looked down. A figure was staring at him from the page with dark, expressionless eyes: a pale horse with a mane of seaweed, coming out of the water. Its mouth was open in a snarl, showing jagged teeth.

Two pages were filled with his grandfather's neat handwriting next to the picture. Mark turned to the cover. The title was carved into the thin rectangle of wood: *The Guide to the Mythology and Mythical Creatures of the British Isles*.

Mark turned back to the page where he had seen the beast and began reading, still not believing his eyes.

Kelpie

The Kelpie is a supernatural shape-shifting water horse that haunts the rivers and streams of Scotland. It is probably one of the best known of Scottish water spirits and is often mistakenly thought to haunt lochs, which are the reserve of the Each Uisge. Yet, different people call the creature by different names and the word KELPIE has been used to describe different water-dwelling spirits. In some regions of Scotland the same beast is called by different names: the Shoopiltee and Nuggle of Shetland and the Tangie of Orkney. In other parts of the United Kingdom, they include the Welsh Ceffyl Dŵr and the Manx Cabbyl-Ushtey

The creature could take many forms and has an insatiable appetite for humans; its most common guise is that of a beautiful tame horse standing by the riverside – a tempting ride for a weary traveller. Anybody foolish enough to mount the horse – perhaps a stranger unaware of the local traditions – would find themselves in dire peril, as the horse would rear and charge headlong into the deepest part of the water, submerging with a noise like thunder to the travellers' watery grave. The Kelpie is also said to warn of impending storms by wailing and howling, which would carry on through the tempest.

Kelpies also have the ability to transform themselves into non-equine forms, and can take on the outward appearance of human figures. In their human form, kelpies are almost invariably male. One of the few stories describing the creature in female form is set at Conon House in Ross and Cromarty. It tells of a 'tall woman dressed in green', with a 'withered, meagre countenance, ever dis-

torted by a malignant scowl', who overpowered and drowned a man and a boy after she jumped out of a stream.

Kelpies can also use their magical powers to summon up a flood in order to sweep a traveller away to a watery grave. The sound of a Kelpie's tail entering the water is said to resemble that of thunder. And if you are passing by a river and hear an unearthly wailing or howling, take care: it could be a Kelpie warning of an approaching storm.[1]

Mark finished reading, put the book away and looked at Tandi. She looked perplexed. So did he, he guessed.

'So this is what we're seeing?' Tandi asked. 'Scottish water ghosts?'

'But this doesn't make any sense!' Mark said. 'We're not in Scotland. How can they be here, in Birmingham?'

He thought about it more. *Kelpie.* It was not the first time he had heard the name. But if he had heard it before, then where?

And suddenly he knew. It was so simple – the answer was right in front of him. He looked down at the book and at his grandfather's handwriting.

'My grandpa was Scottish,' he said.

'What?'

---

[1] Sources:
http://www.mysteriousbritain.co.uk/scotland/folklore/kelpie.html
http://www.historic-uk.com/CultureUK/The-Kelpie/
https://en.wikipedia.org/wiki/Kelpie

'My grandfather. He was Scottish. And he told me about them.'

'He told you about the Kelpies?'

'Yes. When I was little. He told me about ghostly horses that live in the water and drown people. But I still don't understand why I see them.'

'My auntie once told me,' Tandi said, 'that when people travel, the stories that belong to their nation and their culture travel, too. Your grandfather came to Birmingham from Scotland – he brought his Scottish stories with him.'

'But how come you see them as well?' Mark asked. 'Do you know anyone Scottish?'

'Actually, I do. Well, not personally. But my auntie told me that when my family were in Jamaica, they had a white pastor in the church there. He was Scottish.'

'But surely the pastor wouldn't talk about mythical creatures,' Mark said.

'My auntie told me he did. We have our own stories. A lot of people in Jamaica believe in God and at the same time they believe in ghosts or duppies. One of the duppies is believed to be a three-legged horse. This belief is more of a folk tale, like a superstition, and the pastor would say in his sermons that the different peoples had their own stories about ghostly creatures and that people shouldn't believe in superstitions.'

'So you think that all of this is the reason why we see them?'

'I don't have any better explanation,' Tandi said. 'But I know this for sure, and I believe in it – stories travel further than storytellers.'

'Does that mean someone else can see them as well?'

'Yes. And we don't know when we'll see them again.'

'Doesn't that scare you?' Mark asked.

'It does,' Tandi replied. 'But I can't be afraid all my life. Otherwise, I'd never leave the house.'

'You're right.' Mark nodded in agreement.

'You know what?' Tandi said suddenly. 'You're tough.'

'What do you mean?' Mark asked.

'You fought them. You fought for me. Don't think I don't understand what that means.'

And she hugged him tight. It seemed that she'd never let go. Not that Mark wanted her to.

Part Three

August-September

Chapter 24

Sarah

Sarah took a huge pile of entangled bed linen and clothes from the washing machine.

'George, come and help me, please' she called. Unfortunately, there was only one man in the house now to help her. Mark had gone to a school camp. It was a science camp in the countryside not far from Birmingham where the students went together with the teachers to learn more about the world around them and to play sports and have fun at the same time. She liked the fact that Mark went to these – she would have liked to have the chance to go when she was his age.

George came down and Sarah handed him the basket with the washing and said:

'Take it out to the garden and hang it out to dry, will you?'

Sarah wanted to catch up with all of the housework while Mark was away at the camp. She also would have liked to spend more time alone with George, but unfortunately he couldn't take time off at the same time as Mark was away. Still, George's holidays would start in a couple of days' time. They would have enough time to catch up.

'You sure you're feeling okay?' George asked, nodding at her belly. 'I should be emptying the machine, not you.'

'Yes, I'm fine,' she said. 'A little bit of exercise won't harm me.'

Her mind went back to that weekend in July when they all went out as a family. She felt happier that day than she had felt in the past year. Things seemed to be getting back to normal. Yet, there was a feeling of unease that didn't let go of her. It all seemed too good to be true, she thought suspiciously.

'You're being stupid,' Mary Beth said to her when George disappeared through the back door into the garden. 'Things are fine. What is it that you don't like?'

'I don't know,' Sarah said with a sigh. 'Perhaps I'm just being stupid. I'm just scared that this won't last.'

'What won't last?'

'George not drinking. Us being close again. Mark being happy. I like the fact that he's happy. That he's got a girlfriend who is a good friend and understands him. All of this looks so... so fragile.'

'You remember how George reacted when you told him that his son likes a girl and even fought for her?'

Sarah did. Her husband had pounded the air with his fist, grinning victoriously, and said, 'I knew the boy was hiding something! Just friends, he said. Just friends, my foot!'

'It was your effort that put your family back together,' Mary Beth said firmly.

'And God's help, too,' Sarah added.

'Yes,' Mary Beth agreed. 'And God's help, too. It's not fragile.'

'Maybe not. But the work is not finished.'

'Is it ever?' Mary Beth asked. Sarah knew that her imaginary friend was right. The ringing of the phone interrupted her thoughts. Sarah went into the hall and picked up the receiver.

'Hello?' she said.

'Sarah? Is that you?'

'Yes, it's me.' She struggled to recognise the voice. 'Who am I speaking to?' she asked.

'It's Father Grahame Clifton,' the voice said. Of course! The vicar from her foster family.

'Sarah, child,' Father Grahame said, his voice full of concern. 'I've got some sad news for you. Sister Margaret, your group leader at the old orphanage, has passed away.'

'What?' Sarah asked. 'When?' Suddenly she felt weak and the walls around her swayed. She held onto the wall to support herself.

'Last night. I know she was very dear to you.'

'Yes,' Sarah said, quietly, 'she was. We were in touch. How did it happen?'

'She had cancer. Never told anyone, only the vicar in her convent. Do you know where she lived?'

'Yes, Holy Cross Convent in Loughborough. I would like to come to the funeral.'

'Of course. Can you get there?'

'I could come to Loughborough or Leicester by train, but I'm not sure how to go from there.'

'I've got a car,' Father Grahame said. 'I could meet you in Leicester and give you a lift.'

'Alright,' Sarah said. 'Thank you very much.'

She hung up and went into the garden. George had just finished with the washing. Sarah went up to him, put her arms around his shoulders and pressed her face to his chequered shirt. George hugged her back.

'What is it?' he whispered into her hair. Sarah tried to fight back tears.

'Father Grahame just called,' she said, wiping her eyes. 'Sister Margaret's passed away.'

Sarah thought about her time at the orphanage. Sister Margaret's radiant image stood out against the grey walls in her memories. Sarah's brightest memories of the nun were her sewing classes. This was where Sarah had learnt what she liked best. Sister Margaret was very skilled with a needle: her embroidered tablecloths decorated all of the tables in the orphanage; her white lacework looked like it was made of snow and ice.

'She taught me almost everything I can do with my hands,' Sarah said. Tears started running down her cheeks and dripping into the soft fabric of George's shirt.

'Where will the funeral be?' George asked.

'In Loughborough, in the convent where she lived after the orphanage closed. I'll need to go away for a couple of days.'

'I'm sorry to hear about her,' George said. 'When you come back, I'll be at home with anything you need.'

'Thank you,' Sarah whispered, hugging George tightly. 'I need to start getting ready,' she said, reluctantly pulling away from him. 'I still need to call Father Grahame and arrange a time for him to pick me up.'

Chapter 25

Mark

Mark filled two tin buckets under the tap, set them on the ground and got ready to carry them back to the camp. It was his turn to do the dishes that evening, so he'd need to put the buckets onto the hot ashes of their campfire to heat the water up. They had grilled meat for dinner, so the dishes were going to be greasy.

The camp, where has was staying with some other boys from his school, was at the end of a farmer's field. They had already been there for five days. It was a science camp and they spent most of the time exploring the surrounding nature, watching wildlife and conducting experiments with their science teachers. The biology teacher seemed to be having a really great time, using every opportunity to explain something about the nature around them. Mark felt sorry it was not Mrs Blake who had gone with them – he found her lessons quite interesting. But then, he couldn't imagine Mrs Blake sleeping under a tent, no matter how comfortable it was.

The weather had been exceptionally hot all week. Mark and his classmates had spent quite a lot of time outside, and there were many fun activities besides the learning. On the whole, Mark was enjoying himself quite a lot. He especially liked the game called 'The Fox Hunt'. It was played at night with torches. Several main players, the 'foxes', were meant to hide in the forest and the other players, the 'hunters', had to find them using their torches and catch them. The game ended once all the 'foxes' had been caught. They played it on two of the five nights they had spent there and everyone tried very hard because the best 'fox' and the best 'hunter' would be given a prize.

Still, there were things that he missed. One of them, of course, was talking to Tandi. Her school camp was earlier in the summer, in July, and now she was simply staying at home in Birmingham. Another thing he missed was his factory. He had replaced the lock and Tandi had helped him tidy up, but he couldn't get rid of the feeling that there was some *other* presence in the place. Mark felt the need to go through it properly and put everything in its place.

And there was something else that didn't allow him to enjoy his stay in peace. He saw that hideous beast again. He hoped he had imagined it. He tried to convince himself that he had, but with little success.

The night before, in the forest, as they were playing 'The Fox Hunt', he had sped down a narrow path winding among the ancient pines, leaving the others behind. He was getting better at running, especially since he had started walking Spot together with Tandi and volunteered to exercise with him in early July. Spot needed a lot of exercise (Tandi said that otherwise, he would turn into a real pig with his appetite) and Mark would run out of breath very fast the first few times, but as he did it more and more often, he was able to run for longer periods and started to enjoy it a lot. This time, as he sped down the small dirt path with only a small torch to light his way, he had an indescribable sense of freedom. There was only him and the excitement of the night. Mark had missed this feeling. The gentle breeze of the night was tousling his hair and cooling his sweaty face, and he felt as if all his muscles were working in harmony.

And then, suddenly, as he shone his torch forwards, something appeared in the spotlight about fifteen yards away. A pearly-white shape; a beast with four limbs. A mane of dark green on its head and neck; outlines of powerful muscles under the hide.

And, although it was too far away to be seen clearly, Mark saw two black pits in its eye sockets. The darkness in them was beyond scary. It was the darkness of the grave.

Mark stopped in his tracks. The creature stood in the spotlight for about two seconds, eyeing him, and then it opened its mouth and let out a sound. This sound wasn't the kind a horse makes. It wasn't the kind of sound any animal would make. It was not a neigh, not a whinny but a desolate cry, like a howl or a hoot, coming from the chest of the most miserable being in the world. It made Mark's hair stand on end.

Suddenly, Mark heard a rustling sound in the bushes nearby. He almost jumped at the sound, flashing the light at the source. Mark sighed with relief: it was one of the 'foxes'. The boy shot out of the spotlight, jumped over the low-growing bush and disappeared into the thickets. Mark dashed after him and whistled, calling other 'hunters'. As he started running, he shone the torch at the same spot again, but the beast was no longer there. He kept running, but the feeling of freedom was gone. Instead, it was fear that drove him forwards. Inexplicable, almost animal fear. He had to get closer to the others. He knew what those creatures were capable of.

Mark still wondered what had happened when he fought them and fell into the canal. Why did they attack him? No matter how many times he thought about it, he still had no idea. It made no sense to him. The horses certainly knew he could see them. Tandi could see them too. Did they know that? Probably they did. Was he seeing something he wasn't supposed to see? Were they afraid that he and Tandi would start talking about it? This seemed plausible, but if they hadn't attacked them, they would have never told each other that they could see them.

Mark brought the buckets of water back to the camp. The fire had gone out and there was a pile of hot ashes and embers left in its place, surrounded by a circle of bricks and stones. His classmate Joshua, who was also on washing-up duty, was arranging the dirty pots and plates and pouring washing-up liquid over them.

'Come on!' Joshua said, scrubbing a plate with a wire sponge. 'Why is it us that have to wash up when everyone's having roast meat for supper, eh?'

Mark looked at Joshua. He wasn't really complaining; he was smiling. Mark returned the smile.

'Just be glad we don't have to do the work in the rain,' he said as he set one of the buckets on the pile of hot ashes and embers, taking care not to let it lean over.

'I wouldn't mind some heavy rain,' Joshua said. 'Then we could just, you know, squirt washing-up liquid over all this stuff and leave it outside. It would be better than any dishwasher!'

'Be careful what you wish for,' Mark said, looking at the sky. 'I think the weather is back to normal again and we're going to pay for the nice weather we've had.'

The sky was beginning to look nasty. The sun was sinking behind the forest in the west and storm clouds were coming from the east. Dark grey and almost black, they were swirling, bumping into one another and advancing like an angry mob. There would certainly be a storm later that night.

'Let's hurry up,' Joshua said. 'I don't want to be caught out in the storm.'

'Hurry up, indeed!' called a voice behind them. Mark turned – it was Mr Blackpool, their chemistry teacher. 'Have you been paying attention in my classes, gentlemen? If you want to heat the water, there's a faster way to do it. That way, you can definitely finish before the storm comes.'

'What, cover it up with something, sir?' Joshua guessed.

'That's a correct answer, Powell, but I'm not a physics teacher. This is a mechanical way. There is a chemical way, too. Think, lads, what can you do with water to make it boil faster?'

Mark thought carefully and then an idea came to him.

'Salt, sir. Salty water boils faster.'

'Well done, Davies. Good thinking – bonus points for you. See you later, lads,' Mr Blackpool said and disappeared into the teachers' tent.

'I'll go fetch some salt,' Mark said. He went towards the middle of their camp where all the food supplies were. He was starting to feel the wind coming from the fields towards the forest. The wind was bringing the storm clouds closer. As the clouds approached, Mark started feeling uneasy. This had nothing to do with the storm: he was never afraid of the thunder or the dark. He enjoyed exploring dark places and when he was a child, loud noises excited him. This was something else. It could have had something to do with the vision he had had the night before... but had he really seen it? Or had it just been his imagination playing tricks on him, a game of light and shadows in the night? It had been too brief to know for sure.

A sudden gust of wind made Mark shudder. He squatted down at the entrance to the tent, unzipped it and found a bag of salt. He took it, zipped the entrance back up and stood up to return to the dishes before going to his tent to fetch his hoodie. Mark looked in the direction of the forest.

And there it stood.

Covered by the long shadows of the pines that grew on the outer edge of the forest, lurking in between the trees was the horse. Its unblinking eyes were looking fixedly at him. Mark wanted to call these eyes 'empty', but they were not. They were full of hatred, hatred like he'd never seen before. This hatred transformed all its features. The horse opened its snarling jaws, revealing a bloodied mouth with jagged teeth inside. The same bloodied mouth from his dream that had sung in a voice like that of a cackling jackal:

Georgie Porgie pudding and pie,
Your daddy made your mummy cry.
Your daddy's bound to rot in hell,
But you'll be joining him as well!

Mark felt his fingers shake as a wave of nausea washed over him. He clenched his fists to control the shivering.

Something was happening, he sensed it. He saw those creatures for a reason. Something was happening at home. He had to get there. He had to get home as soon as possible.

Mark had never felt so angry at those pale creatures, nor had he felt so determined. He glanced at his wristwatch. It was a quarter to nine. His mind went into overdrive. He had around thirty-five minutes. At twenty past nine, there would be a train. This train would take him to Birmingham.

As Mark was returning to the end of the camp where Joshua was waiting for him with the dishes, he tried to calm his breathing and calculated the time it would take him to get to the railway station. It was over forty minutes on foot. He would need to leave as soon as possible and run. The only thing was, he had to leave without being noticed in order not to raise any suspicions. Leaving the camp without an accompanying teacher was not allowed.

Mark came to the bucket, took off the piece of plywood that Joshua had used to cover it and dropped three fistfuls of salt into the water.

'That should be enough,' he said. Then he took a pot from the pile of dishes and started scrubbing it, trying to get rid of the soot and bits of burnt food that had stuck to the bottom. As soon as he had finished with the pot, Mark said to Joshua:

'Hey, mate, I need to go to the loo. Stay here till I'm back, will you?'

'Okay, no problem, Mark,' Joshua replied. Mark went towards his tent, grabbed his black hoodie and pulled it on. Then he took a path towards the forest, as if to go to the toilet. The clouds had covered the entire sky and more were coming. Darkness was descending on the forest and the fields. Cold wind was whirling around Mark.

Lightning flashed in the darkness – weakly, like the flash of a camera. The first rumble of thunder rolled from across the fields.

Mark saw this as a call to action. He sprinted around the edge of the forest and turned into a path between two farmers' fields. There was another thunderclap, this time nearer, and large raindrops began falling from the black clouds. Mark ran faster as the rain intensified. In his mind, he could only see one thing: the creature's face, its bloodied cackling mouth twisted in a grimace of hatred and eyes like the darkest caves the human mind could imagine.

The forest behind him howled and creaked like an enormous beast awakening. Mark ran faster still, feeling his muscles tighten and relax with every stride. Once again, he was grateful for the running practice he had had. As he thought of the horses more and more, it was not fear that filled his chest and made him run but hatred. These creatures – Kelpies, or whatever they were – had stolen his peace. They had stolen the peace of his family. They were stealing his family from him, too. His hatred for them and anger at them burned inside him, forcing him to run faster. The wind was whipping at his clothes; the hood of his jumper, his hair and face were all soaked – Mark didn't notice any of this. He had to run and make it to the railway station. His jeans were soaking wet at the front, too, and the thick fabric slowed down his movement. Despite his training with Spot, Mark was beginning to slow down. His anger-induced run had used up a lot of energy. A dull, uncomfortable ache was starting to throb in his side and it was hard to breathe.

Across the vast fields that lay in front of him, in the darkness of the coming night, Mark suddenly saw the headlights of the last train of the day as it exited from the tunnel, ready to pull into the station in less than three minutes' time. His muscles were already aching from the effort as he prepared himself for the final spurt. He needed to run faster or he'd never make it.

In his hurry, Mark didn't notice a bundle of tangled wire that was lying in a patch of tall grass in the middle of the dirt road.

His feet slipped as he tripped and tumbled forwards with his arms outstretched.

Chapter 26

George

It was about six o'clock when the storm started. George thought it rather strange – it had been a very sunny week, and a stiflingly hot one, too. Then, all of a sudden, the clouds shrouded the sky and everything turned so dark. The wind made the tree branches on their street sway dangerously and ripped at the leaves, as if threatening to strip the trees naked.

George was sitting in the armchair in the living room with a blanket over his feet. For some time, he flicked through the TV channels, but saw that there was nothing to watch and turned the TV off. He got up and began pacing the floor anxiously, looking for something to do. Perhaps some DIY? How about fixing that shelf in the corner? Sarah had told him a couple of days before that the screws had become a bit loose and the shelf was moving up and down. Or perhaps he should cook something? Sarah would be coming back this evening. He'd taken some days off to spend alone with her. Mark was going to be away at the school camp for another five days, so they could have the entire house to themselves. Unfortunately, Sarah had to go to that funeral, but she'd be back today and they could still spend some quality time together.

George looked out of the window and quickly backed away, drawing the curtains. The storm made him feel uneasy. It was not so much the wind and the rain – after all, he was a builder who spent a lot of time outside and believed that there was no bad weather, only bad clothing. It was the darkness that made him feel uneasy. It brought back the worst memories – those of his father.

Once, when he was seven, his father had punished him by locking him in the basement. He couldn't remember what he'd done – punishment was too frequent for him to keep track of the details. His father was drunk, too, so it could have been anything that annoyed him.

There was a small cupboard that always smelt of damp and mould. George's father shut him in that cupboard and locked the door. The boy spent the entire day there, shivering from the cold, crying and begging for forgiveness, hoping that his father would hear him. His mother tried to sneak into the basement and smuggle in some food for him, but his father caught her at it. He pulled George out of the cupboard by the collar of his shirt and whipped him with a cane in front of his mother. When she tried to protect him, he backhanded her across the face and punched her in the stomach several times. She vomited on the floor and his father recoiled in disgust. Then he pushed George back into the cupboard and locked him there till the next morning.

George shuddered at the memory. The house now seemed bitterly cold and dark to him, so he turned on the lights and the heating. He wrapped a blanket around himself and sat on the floor with his back to the heater – something he hadn't done in years, since he was a child. Yet, the shivering would not go away.

'It was after that incident that your mother decided to leave your father forever,' Rahab said. 'She fell when he punched her and broke her wrist.'

George looked up at Rahab who was sitting on the floor before him.

'Yes, I remember that,' he said with a nod. 'That was when my life changed. Even if I wasn't able to connect fully to my new… my new father. My real father. Thank you, Rahab.'

George extended his hand and Rahab shook it.

'You're most welcome. I have chosen you. I had to protect you.'

'May I ask you…' George began, suddenly feeling timid. 'Why… why do you wear a mask?'

'Why are masks worn in general, George?'

'For disguise. To hide one's face.'

'Correct, George. Disguise. You see, I do not reveal myself to just anyone. I reveal myself to those who recognise me. For you have not chosen me, I have chosen you. You recognised me against all the odds. Two thousand years ago, it was very hard to recognise the Creator of all galaxies in that dusty carpenter from Galilee who spoke with a strong regional accent – and yet some did. Talking about carpenters – what an honourable trade! Chris McRae was a carpenter, wasn't he?'

'He was. A very good one. Half of the furniture in this place was made by him,' George said. Why couldn't he stop shivering? Rahab looked at him attentively.

'I think you might be falling ill, George.'

'No,' George said abruptly. 'I'm probably just cold and tired.'

'And stressed,' Rahab added. 'Remember, I know your heart and I am aware of what you're going through. But you should not reject the idea of falling ill so fiercely, George. Falling ill is not the same as being ill. When something is starting, you can nip it in the bud. But it's not the heater you need. You need to get warm on the inside, if you know what I mean.'

George stood up and looked outside. The rain was hammering through the blackness. As if guessing his thoughts, Rahab said:

'What is more important to you, George – staying dry or staying healthy?'

George knew the answer to this. He pulled on his coat, still shivering, ran outside to a nearby off-licence and bought two bottles of whiskey. He returned home, poured himself a large glass and swallowed it in two gulps. The liquid ran down his throat, settling in his stomach with a familiar warming feeling. Finally, he stopped shivering. With a steady hand, George poured himself another glass and gulped it down, faster than the previous one. The fuzzy warmth spread through his body. He sat on the sofa and poured himself another one.

'So, George, where has your wife gone?' Rahab asked.

'To a funeral. She grew up in an orphanage, as you know, and was schooled by nuns. She was quite close to one of them – she passed away and Sarah went to say goodbye to her.'

'I'm sorry, George, but you are only partially right. The funeral is only a convenient pretext.'

George froze in his seat. Rahab knew something.

'Tell me more,' he demanded.

'There are a few things she can do while she's away. Visit her lover, of course – now, as she's pregnant, she can sleep around safely. I mentioned that before. But that's not the only thing. Far from it. There is something much worse. She does not trust you anymore – as a man, or as a husband, or as the father of your son. And the reason for her mistrust is not you – it stems from her own lies and deceitful actions. But she is planning to leave you, George. She will go to a solicitor and file for divorce. Pour yourself another drink, George. I'm going to tell you something very unpleasant.'

George obeyed, as if entranced. He wanted not to believe Rahab's words, he wanted it not to be true. Yet, he remembered who was standing before him and who was speaking to him. It could not be a lie. So it must be the truth. George's hands started shivering again, but the cold had nothing to do with it this time. The bottle was half-empty now. Rahab went towards the table and poured himself a glass, too. He grabbed the glass with his slick black-gloved forelimb and downed it in one.

'Your name will be dragged through the mud,' he said. 'She will take your house and your son. You will live on the streets, George. This is what she wants. She wants to take your life from you. Her lover will sleep in your bed, eat from your plate – or maybe they will buy a new bed and new plates, because secretly she wants to rid herself of every single memory of you!'

'No!' George screamed, pain, anger and desperation swelling inside him and rising like water rises inside a drowning ship. 'I refuse to believe it!'

'I'm sorry, George,' Rahab said. 'I'm only telling you what you've seen yourself. Or maybe you didn't because you were so busy recently, and you trusted your wife, so naïvely. But she betrayed you a long time ago, George. She's stopped sharing her secrets with you. She has become more withdrawn. She is no longer yours. But –' Rahab said, facing George, 'fear not. For both you and I know she must be stopped. And I can help you do it.'

George poured himself more whiskey and sat at the table, eyeing it sombrely. The bottle was almost empty and George opened the second one.

Suddenly, soft footsteps drew his attention. He looked in the direction of the sound and saw another horse figure stepping out of the tall mirror on the wardrobe door. The figure removed her mask. It was Lilith with streaks of fire in her hair, like burning coals. This time, she gave off a smell of burning incense: it seemed to George that she had rubbed it in her hair and now smoke surrounded her, shimmering like some unearthly haze, like a distant nebulous galaxy on the other side of the Universe.

Lilith approached the table and took a swig from the bottle.

'No one can take your life away from you, George,' she said, slipping off her pearly-white robe. 'You'll need strength to fight this battle. Show me how much strength you've got and I'll give you twice that! Let's hurry, though – your wife is coming back tonight.'

'I'll show you,' George whispered, ripping his shirt off. 'There's more than enough time.'

Rahab stood in the corner, a whiskey bottle in his hand, watching George take Lilith as she moaned with pleasure.

'You're quite a warrior, George,' he said, taking a hearty swig.

Chapter 27

Sarah

Sarah tightened the belt of her coat and lifted the collar, shielding herself from the bitter wind. She was coming home from the funeral where she had said her last goodbye to Sister Margaret. The sudden change in the weather shocked her as she got off the train. Rumbling clouds covered the sky, and the wind pierced her thin clothes and flapped the tail of her coat. The streets were wet – it had stopped raining a few minutes before. The weather had gone mad. It was as if the preceding warm and pleasant week simply had not happened. She could not wait to come home, where George was waiting for her. No doubt, he had turned the heating on as well – it was August, but it felt like October.

A bolt of lightning flashed in the distance. The next moment, the rain started hammering down again as if someone had opened all of the taps in the heavens. A small stream formed on the road, by the pavement. Sarah started walking faster, cursing herself for not having taken her umbrella.

As she approached her street and house, a strange feeling of unease started gnawing at her from the inside. She could not tell what it was, and this made her annoyed. Something was troubling her. But what was it? Was it something to do with Mark? He was at that summer camp. He should be okay – if he wasn't, they would have received a phone call. George would have told her, there was a phone available at the funeral. Still, she hoped Mark would not get wet out there in the woods. No, it was something else. But what?

Sarah came to the door and pulled out her keys. She saw that the lights were on in the living room. And there were voices. Was George not alone? She stopped and listened. Silence fell. What was going on? Well, there was only one way to find out.

Sarah inserted the key into the lock and turned it. The feeling of unease grew. She rushed inside the house. She didn't have to see the bottle in George's hand or see the expression on his face. She could sense his state the way people can sense each other after they have lived together for a long time.

'You're drunk!'

Sarah was shocked by the tone of her own voice. There was so much frustration and disappointment in it. George staggered towards her, focussing his eyes on her face. He took a swig from the bottle in his hand, wiped his mouth with his sleeve and stared at her.

'Where have you been?' he demanded. He was drunk on more than whiskey, Sarah observed. He was intoxicated with fury that was flashing in his eyes. Almost instinctively, Sarah wanted to back off, but something inside her told her to stand her ground.

'You know where I've been,' she replied. 'To the funeral. And stop talking to me in that tone. You're drunk and I find it unpleasant talking to you.'

Her voice surprised her again – it was cold, but there was a pleading note and… pity. Pity for this man who was standing before her. He was her *husband* and she was losing the battle for him after thinking that she'd almost won. Something terrible, more terrible and powerful than alcohol was clawing at her husband and taking him away from her and Mark. Raw feelings echoed inside her, rebounding off the bare walls of her soul. But there was also a steely determination to fight inside her, and George sensed it; and he didn't like it at all.

'Oh, sorry to spoil your evening for you,' George said, with a sarcastic drawl in his words. 'You've done so many great things today: you went to the funeral, had a good rough shag with your young stud… So, who is he? Or *they*?'

'What?' Sarah gasped as if he'd slapped her. She could hardly believe her ears. 'Are you accusing me of sleeping with other men?'

'Yes, I fucking am! Don't pretend to be stupid! So, how thick is his dick, huh? Has he managed to rub your unsatisfied bitch-hole?'

He spat out the last sentence like a mouthful of blackened motor oil. For a few moments, Sarah was lost for words. She looked her husband right in the eyes and almost staggered backwards the second time when she saw a menacing shadow flash in his pupils. A shadow that did not belong there. A shadow that should have never been created to roam the earth. Something inside her was telling her to ignore what he'd said, but it took her all her strength to obey that voice.

'George, you should listen to yourself!' Sarah implored. 'You're not being yourself. What's the matter with you?'

'I know what you're up to!' George shouted, flailing the bottle around so that Sarah had to duck to avoid being hit. 'I know what you're plotting against me!'

'What the fuck are you talking about?' Sarah shouted back. She was on the edge of tears. 'George, your drinking will drive me to insanity and you to the grave!'

Fury flashed in George's eyes as he advanced towards Sarah. His own shadow grew taller on the wall behind him. It was black and jagged like a storm cloud.

'No, you sly woman!' he growled. 'It's you who's driving me to the grave. You won't trick me with your fake tears this time. I know what you want!'

Sarah did not recognise her husband anymore. His face was contorted and his hair was standing up belligerently. His lips were twisted in a beastly snarl.

'All I want is to help you!' she shouted, recoiling as he waved his bottle in the air again.

'LIAR! All you want is to take my life from me!'

The bottle flew towards the wall and exploded into a thousand shards. The smell of whiskey pouring over the heater filled the living room. George took a few angry and uneven steps towards Sarah.

'Don't come any closer!' Sarah screamed.

'Stop shouting at me or I will silence you!'

Sarah stopped in her tracks.

'George, please listen to yourself! What are you saying?' she pleaded, tears filling her eyes.

'Yes, silence you! I have the right to silence anyone who is bound to lead me into damnation. I won't let you ruin my life!'

And then something happened that Sarah could never explain afterwards. George was standing a good eight feet away from her, his red face contorted with drunken rage. He could never have reached that far – it wasn't him that hit her. But she felt something hard and bony collide with her stomach.

Right where the baby was.

Then the world turned red and she slumped against the wall.

Chapter 28

Mark

The fall hurt. Mark's outstretched arms hit the wet, slippery clay and slid down the road, his palms and forearms scratching against the small stones in the ground. His body followed, his chest hitting the road first. Mark instinctively rolled onto his side, trying to protect himself from being winded. He succeeded, but his shoulder and ribs took most of the impact instead of his sternum. Mark gasped and yelped in pain. His hands began to smart. His entire front was smeared with mud and clay.

Mark pushed himself up on his arms, trying to get back to his feet. His entire body groaned in protest. He tried to ignore the pain and squinted, looking in the direction of the train. The rain was not heavy, but the visibility was poor and all of his clothes were soaked and soiled, and his shoes waterlogged as he ran across the puddles, not bothering to look where he was stepping. He braced himself, getting ready to sprint, when forked lightning shot across the sky and heavy rain with hailstones started falling.

This is going to hurt, Mark thought as he pumped his arms and started gathering speed, running down the dirt road, thinking only about the train.

Icy raindrops hit him in the face like splashing shrapnel; his shoes splattered across the puddles; the bottoms of his jeans were all caked with liquid mud. He didn't care about his clothes. All that mattered was getting home in time, otherwise he felt that something terrible, something irreversible would happen.

Every breath he took seemed to rip his ribcage apart as piercing pain shot through his side and his bruised ribs screamed for mercy. Mark gritted his teeth and continued running. He crossed the empty station and jumped towards the doors of the train, just in time. The doors bleeped several times to signal that they were closing, and then the train hissed and pulled out of the station, speeding towards Birmingham.

Mark bent down, his hands on his knees, drawing in shuddering breaths. He clutched at his chest, trying to calm down his heart which was hammering against his ribs as if it was about to jump out. Then he remembered that Grandpa Chris had always told him to move when resting after exercising. Stopping suddenly after making a lot of effort was dangerous, he said.

Moving was the last thing Mark wanted to do, but he forced himself to straighten his back and breathe deeply. He looked around the carriage: he was the only passenger there. Apparently, other people had better things to do than travel in this horrible weather.

Mark began walking along the aisle between the rows of seats. He walked down the aisle once, turned around and walked halfway back. His heart and breathing had calmed down and he took a seat. It was incredibly dark outside the window. Too dark for nine o'clock. The clouds and the storm made it look as if night had fallen much earlier. Mark looked into the darkness beyond the window. The rain was still lashing against the glass as the train sped down the tracks towards Kings Norton railway station. His reflection in the glass looked gaunt and pale. Now, as he was sitting on the train, he started feeling cold because of his wet clothes. Luckily, the heating was on. Mark moved closer to the heater, putting his feet in soaked trainers directly onto it. Deep inside, he prayed for the train to hurry up and tried to calm down, but with little success. Something was happening at home, something strange and unfamiliar, something frightening – he sensed it but could not explain to himself what it was and felt he had no control over it.

As soon as the train stopped at Kings Norton, Mark hastily pushed the 'open door' button. There was another run ahead of him, from the station to his house. He jumped out of the doors as soon as they opened and sped down the streets. Dashing down the familiar alleys and around the familiar corners, he arrived at his house. There was a crack between the door and the frame; it was unlocked. Mark kicked the front door open and ran into the living room.

What he saw inside made him stop on the threshold.

His mother was lying on the floor. She was breathing heavily and gasping for air through shuddering sobs. His father was standing several feet away. His face, twisted into a hideous mask of fury, was unrecognisable.

And there were two others. What Mark saw was a little barefoot girl in a white night dress who was holding a red ribbon in her tiny hands. His mother was desperately clutching the other end of the ribbon, which disappeared into her balled fists which she was pressing to her stomach.

And someone else.

Mark froze. He eyed the white overalls, the slick black gloves and the two slimy blotches of black oil in the horse's face. This kind of blackness could only exist in one place in this world – a soul that was damned for eternity.

The horse was holding the red ribbon as well. The soft fabric – or perhaps vapour or mist, whatever the ribbon was made of – was crumpled in the beast's grip and the horse tore at it with its teeth and tried to rip it by wrenching it in all directions. Each time it pulled at the ribbon, its colour became more intense, turning from scarlet to crimson to almost rusty brown. Each time it tore at it, Mark's mother gasped in pain and the little girl screamed in terror.

Mark knew he was the only one who could see and hear what was really happening. But when his gaze shifted towards his father, he started shivering with fear and rage. The position of his father's body and hands was exactly the same as the horse's. His father was tugging, wrenching, ripping, clawing and tearing with his teeth at an invisible scarlet ribbon that was connecting his mother to her unborn baby.

'What are you doing, you bastard!' he shouted. He was not sure whom he was addressing with these words – his father, the horse or both. Seeing his father tear at the invisible ribbon brought a realisation that made him break out in a cold sweat. The actions of the horse and his father were intertwined. When the horse attacked, his father attacked.

Mark realised he only had a few seconds to act. Attacking the horse was out of the question, he knew that – it would evade him, vanishing into smoke and reappearing after he had fallen on the floor, like it did at the canal. There was only one option left.

Mark lunged forwards, jumped up and flung himself onto his father.

I'm very sorry, Dad, he thought. Then he gathered all his strength and speed and struck his own father's temple with his fist.

Chapter 29

Mark

The blow was so strong that the horse figure reeled and backed a step or two, releasing the ribbon. The little girl instantly stopped screaming and ran towards Sarah. Mark's mother was still crouching near the wall, her arms wrapped around her own body, her eyes shut in pain and horror. Mark punched his father in the face. The horse swerved and took two steps back.

The little girl touched Sarah's cheek and embraced her neck with her tiny arms. Sarah returned the embrace and held her unborn daughter close. Circles of light emerged from the lines where their bodies touched. Then Mark saw the girl start to disappear, as if she were stepping or melting into her mother's body. When the last strand of her hair blended with Sarah's own, the circles of light vanished. Sarah gasped for air feverishly. The girl was safely back, and the ribbon of her life was once again strongly intertwined with her mother's.

All the while, the horse watched this all happen with unblinking eyes. As soon as Mark flung himself at his father, the creature seemed to become paralysed, unable to move until the little girl dissolved into

Sarah's body. As soon as Mark's unborn sister was safely back inside her mother's body, the horse screamed in rage, baring its ugly teeth. Mark watched in horror as the horse turned to face him and his father. As he watched it, he lost concentration and his father wriggled from beneath him, pinned him to the ground and hit his head against the floorboards. Dark circles floated before Mark's eyes as pain shot through the back of his head. Mark saw his mother move to look at them, dazed and disoriented.

'Stop it!'

His mother's voice reached him as if through the fog.

'Stop it, both of you!'

I wish I could stop it, Mum, Mark thought as he tried to free himself from his father's grasp. *But if I do, both you and Dad will be dead. You won't understand.*

Mark was suffocating under his father's weight. George did not punch his son. Instead, he strangled him, keeping him pinned to the ground. He weighed five stones more than Mark did, and certainly had a competitive advantage. Mark could smell his father's breath which reeked of drink and something acrid; he saw George's flushed and swollen face a couple of inches away from his own; he saw the blood vessels in his eyes, his bared teeth... He could no longer recognise his father. Without a trace of his former self left in him, all semblance of humanity erased from his face, with fury in his eyes and hatred in the twist of his lips, the man he was fighting had only one task: to kill him.

Fear seized Mark. Fear that was a source of enormous strength. Mark wriggled on the spot and wrenched himself out of his father's grasp. There was a ripping sound and Mark left pieces of his hoodie in his father's hands. Next, with one push, Mark shoved himself away from him. Mark was surprised by the strength of his push – he slid across the floor towards the wall, and his father staggered a couple of yards in the opposite direction, then lost his balance and fell with a crash. Mark saw the horse figure turn away from his mother altogether and fling itself onto his father. It hoisted him up by the collar onto his unsteady feet.

'Get up!' it screeched. 'Get up and fight! This is not the fight I expect from a man who serves me!'

Then, all of a sudden, he flung Mark's father back to the floor.

'Mark, George, what's going on?' his mother screamed behind him.

'Fuck you all!' George shouted back, getting up.

With these words, he ran through the front door that had been open since Mark came in and disappeared into the rain.

'George!' his mother called after him, pleading. Then she suddenly slumped to the floor, her eyes closing.

Mark felt torn: his immediate instincts told him he had to follow his father, but he had to make sure his mother was safe.

'Mum!' He touched her hand. She didn't respond. He jumped towards the table, grabbed a glass of water from the top and splashed it in her face. This worked. His mother opened her eyes. He knelt beside her and glanced around the room. There were only the two of them: the horse figure was gone. She was safe. He had to be with his father now. Mark jumped to his feet and darted towards the door.

'Mark, what's going on?' his mother asked with tears in her eyes. 'Where are you going?'

'I'll explain later,' he said. 'Are you feeling alright? I must go. Stay here, I'll find Dad.'

'Mark, why did you attack your father?'

'Later, Mum, please.' Mark was starting to feel desperate. He had to get outside as soon as possible. 'Stay safe. I've got to stop them.'

'Stop who? Mark!'

But Mark was already outside, in the storm. Just before leaving, he glanced back and saw that his mother had closed her eyes from exhaustion. He shut the door behind him.

Chapter 30

Sarah

Sarah lay on her side, unable to stop the tears streaming from her eyes. The sobs were shaking her body violently, uncontrollably, and she was shivering on the outside and inside. Her mind failed to comprehend what had just happened, what she had just experienced and *seen* with her very eyes.

Her thoughts turned back to her husband and son, bringing pangs of headache. Where were they? Sarah was unable to erase the image from her mind: her husband and her son, the men she loved more than anything in the world, fighting on the floor... as if it was not them.

And what happened before! Her loving George, the only man she trusted enough to tell him everything, changing beyond recognition in an instant. The warm lines of his face twisting into frosty, alien features as if they had been hewn from a piece of rock... and his eyes... His shining, living eyes – they had turned into empty black sockets devoid of all warmth and life in them. Like blotches of black shoe polish. His face was nothing but a repulsive mask of death – it showed existence with no afterlife, no hope, like a tomb of stagnant, stinky underground waters; like the gaping jaws of an abyss.

She felt as if she had looked into the pits of hell.

But what had happened between George's face changing and Mark bursting in? There was something she could not quite comprehend. She was not sure if she had imagined it or whether it was merely a hallucination brought on by the pain, or perhaps she was simply going crazy.

Sarah shuddered violently at the thought as she recalled the stabbing, searing pain in her stomach. She was really scared that she would lose the baby then. Something inside her – something that only mothers can hear – told her she was safe. *Both of them* were safe. But the thought of losing her little girl was so unbearable that Sarah curled into a ball on the floor, hugging her belly protectively, and wanted to howl until her throat hurt.

The pain from the impact was gone, but the memory of it still echoed inside her body, spreading through her blood, flesh and bones like poison. She could not stop shaking. Sarah tried to compose herself and make sense of the situation. What had really happened? Both George's feet were on the ground. So it was not he who had kicked her. Who was it, then? Or *what?*

It sounded ridiculous, but she felt as if she had encountered something... out of this world, something that was ancient and sinister and full of hatred towards all living things. Fear filled her, welling inside her like icy, dirty water. She had to get up. Now! She tried to raise herself using her arms for support. As if mocking her, her arms refused to obey and she immediately collapsed back onto the floor. She felt so small and weak and she hated it. She bloody hated it! Her husband and son were out there, in the storm, and goodness knows what was happening to them, and she was there, lying sprawled on the floor. This was not the behaviour she would expect from herself.

Fear inside her was now mixed with anger. Boiling, bubbling anger that gave her strength. She groaned as with one mighty push she brought herself to her knees. The movement sent her head spinning and black dots danced before her eyes. She was shivering and panting. Sarah raised her head, casting a glance at the door. The white landline phone was hanging on the wall in the hall. She had to get to it. Something that only mothers can feel told her she had to go outside and find Mark and George. And there was no way she could make it alone.

Sarah put her hands together. She needed all the help she could get.

'Please, God,' she prayed. 'Help me.'

A sudden burst of anger surged through her body, giving her enough strength to push herself up and take three unsteady steps. Then her knees treacherously gave way and she had to grab the wall again to prevent herself from falling. *Steady. Steady. Catch your breath.*

'Please,' she whispered. 'Once more, please.'

Another effort of explosive strength... the white flash inside her head almost blinded her for a second. She reached towards the phone and clutched at the receiver as strength left her again. Blackness! Scary blackness, like she had seen in George's eyes.

She waited for her breathing to slow down, reached up again and punched in Jo Blake's number.

'Please,' she prayed again. 'Please, God, let her be at home.'

Four painful double beeps later, she heard:

'Jo Blake's house.'

Sarah lifted her eyes towards the ceiling and mouthed:

'Thank you.'

Then she said into the receiver:

'Jo, this is Sarah. Something terrible has happened. You must come to my house immediately.'

'Coming right now,' the response came. Sarah was grateful for the fact that Jo asked no questions. She hung up and dialled 999.

'Police, ambulance or fire brigade?' the lady on the phone said.

'Ambulance,' Sarah said. 'And police. My husband...' she paused, thinking what exactly she wanted to say. 'He's had a fight. My son is with him.'

'Where are they?'

Sarah paused. She didn't know. But something inside her told her the possible answer. Was that really where they were?

'Madam?' the lady on the phone said. 'Are you there?'

Sarah had no other options. It was either guess or say nothing.

'Yes,' she said. 'They're at the canal in Kings Norton. Follow Primrose Hill and Masshouse Lane.'

'What's your address, madam?'

Sarah gave her address and hung up. She folded her hands in prayer once more this evening. She prayed for strength. She felt she would really need it tonight.

Chapter 31

Mark

Mark was speeding down the street. All his clothes were wet from before, which impeded his movement. He looked anxiously in all directions, peering through the endless curtain of the water and cloudy darkness. Suddenly, something white flashed in the distance to his left. The horse figure. And another one. His father was there, and the creatures were following him.

Mark dashed off in a frantic sprint. The road led down the hill; the blurred lights in the windows shone through the rain. Suddenly, Mark knew where his father was running to. He forced his muscles to make more effort. His ribcage felt as if it was on fire. The horses moved faster and faster, which meant that the distance between him and his father was also increasing.

Suddenly, he saw a man standing in the rain. He stood, surrounded by the storm, his arms raised towards the skies. Two lightning bolts flashed one after another and illuminated him for a split second. Mark would have recognised his white robe and rope belt anywhere.

UNDER THE DARK WATER

'Oak!' Mark shouted. His voice ended in a croak as his lungs were bursting to meet his need for air. The old man turned around with an expression of anxiety on his face.

'My father,' Mark panted. 'He needs help. Over there, quick!' he gasped, pointing towards the dark waters of the canal. Oak nodded and started running, overtaking him.

'Let's go,' he shouted to Mark over his shoulder, trying to overpower the storm. It took Mark much more effort to start running again after he had stopped. He sped after Oak, surprised at the old man's vigour and the ease with which he moved.

And then he saw them. His father was standing on the bank of the canal, with two horse figures on either side of him. He was sure that these figures were the same ones that had attacked him on the bridge several weeks earlier. He still had no idea how to fight them — his fists would go through them as if they were made of fog. Were both of them now connected to his father? Who would he have to attack — his father or the horses?

Oak was thirty yards ahead of him. He ran onto the bank of the canal and stopped a couple of yards away from the scene. Mark saw one of the horses grab his father by the throat with its slick gloved limb and fling him towards the ground.

'Dad! No!' he screamed, rushing towards the scene. Oak stood dumbfounded and watched what was happening. The old man's arms hung limply at his sides.

He can't see them, Mark thought. *He has no idea what is going on.*

Mark rushed past Oak towards his father, but suddenly he felt a sharp kick below his left knee and a blow to his neck as he ran into the old man's outstretched arm. Falling forwards onto the ground, Mark managed to extend his arms in front of him. He fell on the wet gravel, grazing his elbow and the heels of both hands for the second time that night.

'Stop your futile efforts,' Oak said, without looking at him. His Scottish accent was gone. Instead, his guttural voice was not like anything Mark had heard before. His accent seemed to come from another world, not another country. 'Your fool of a father can't be helped.'

With these words, he approached George, who was battling in vain against the horses. The man flailed his arms around, trying to hit someone or something, but his fists only went through the horse figures' bodies, just like Mark's had done. Suddenly, Mark felt a strong grip on the collar of his jacket. He was hauled onto his feet and then his arms were locked behind his back in an iron grip.

'Stop wriggling, you little shit, or I will break your miserable neck,' the voice said in his ear. Mark cast a cautious sideways glance and met the empty gaze from a blotch of oily shoe polish.

One of the horses had left his father's side and was now holding him.

'Rahab, Lilith – well done,' Oak said, addressing the horses. 'Hello, George,' he added, turning to Mark's father.

Then, just as lightning flashed again, Oak kicked Mark's father in the stomach and pushed him into the water. George fell backwards with a scream. Then there was a splash.

'Dad!' Mark shouted over the wind and rain, twisting and jerking his body, fruitlessly trying to free himself from the steely clutches. 'What the fuck are you doing?!' he screamed at Oak. The old man did not even turn to look at him.

Several seconds later, which seemed to Mark like an eternity, there was a scream:

'What the hell is this?' His father emerged on the surface of the water, shaking and spluttering. Mark didn't know how deep the canal was, but it was more than two yards from the edge of the brick-rimmed bank to the water, and probably several yards down to the bottom.

'You will die today, George!' Oak said, looking down at Mark's father. 'My servants will drown you in these waters.'

George splashed his arms, battling against the water. He seemed to have regained his self-awareness.

'You saved my son's life!' he shouted. 'Not even two months ago!' he spluttered. Mark's father was not a bad swimmer, but the alcohol and his soaked clothes and boots were pulling him down. 'Why are you taking mine?'

'Because I can,' Oak replied. 'And because you deserve it! Yes, I saved your son's pitiful life!' Oak shouted back. 'I do not kill innocent souls – especially those whom I know I can't corrupt. Your son can see my horses, George, just as you have been able to recently.'

What? Dad can see those hideous beasts, too?

'But Mark has always seen them. Yes, George, he started seeing them the day you started drinking. They are only workers, simple minds, and your son can see right through them. He will never succumb to their power... but *you* have, and you deserve to die!'

Mark didn't notice the rain lashing at his face anymore. His head was spinning and there was a deafening roar in his ears, like a plane's engine at takeoff. *Oak knows Mark can see them! He can see them, too! And he claims the beasts belong to him.*

Mark's thoughts returned to the night Oak had saved him and he had that bizarre dream. He thought about a disfigured jagged shadow... about its broken back, as of it had fallen from an enormous height... According to local rumours, Oak had fallen from a height before becoming who he was. *The boy dies when I say he dies!* Mark couldn't believe it. Oak, his harmless neighbour was the master of the ghostly horses. Mark's head was spinning and he had to muster all his willpower to remain focused. Something inside him was telling him to distract Oak, to hold his attention.

'It was you!' Mark shouted at him. 'You ransacked my place at the factory!'

'I did!' Oak replied, turning to him. 'But I was not able to find the book by your grandfather where he explained what you're seeing. My servants have also sensed the danger. Both you and that girl can see them. They thought that in time you'd figure out your father can see them too, that you might somehow help your father become free of their influence... and they decided to kill you. But you should not die. For if you die, you will go towards the light. Your father, however, belongs to us. He is damned!'

Both horses – the one standing next to Oak and the one holding Mark – pulled off their masks. The one standing behind Mark stepped in front of him, but his hands remained in an invisible grip.

Mark looked at the beasts facing him and felt as if he was going to be sick. There were two of them under the masks – a man and a woman. The lonely streetlamp illuminated their faces... if they could even be called faces. Leathery parchment was their skin; their noses were flat, snakelike, almost absent; and the same eyes as in their horse masks – no whites, only black, oily blotches. Both the man and the woman had manes of long, greasy hair; the man's head was half-bald, and raw-coloured skin seemed to be tightly pressed against his skull where the hair was missing.

'Do you recall me, George?' the man asked. 'I am Rahab. Not the man who saved you from the river. Not Jesus from the painting of your childhood. Just Rahab, a being with a single purpose – to take lives away. They call me the harbinger of glorified violence. We've had quite a lot of that, haven't we? I can't believe you swallowed everything I told you. I made you so enraged when I told you about your wife cheating on you! As if she would ever have the brains to do that.'

'You're talking about my mother, you shit!' Mark yelled, and he tried to lunge forwards again, only to be held back by a shot of pain through his shoulder as he nearly dislocated it. He gasped in pain and wanted to sink to his knees, but whatever force was holding him now, it kept him upright. He was helpless against it.

'And me, George?' the woman shrieked with laughter. 'Do you remember me? What a nice time we had together! You've got quite a nice cock – it even seems a pity to kill you now.' She emitted a loud, jubilatory cackle.

'We *own* you, George,' Oak shouted. 'We own you and tonight we shall claim you. You've committed the most horrible crime, George: you've just killed your unborn daughter. Your wife hasn't got long left to live, either.'

A roar of thunder shook the sky.

'No! No! Please, I never wanted that!' George shrieked, struggling to grasp at the walls of the canal. But his hands slipped at the last moment and he fell back into the murky water.

'That's a dirty lie! Don't believe him, Dad!'

George looked at his son. It seemed as if he had become aware of his presence for the first time. Mark's name formed on his lips…

'Silence, you unworthy filth!' Oak screamed at Mark. Then he jumped towards him, swung his hand back and struck him across the ear. The blow was so strong that Mark lost his vision for a moment. His ears were ringing and several seconds passed before he heard the next words that Oak uttered:

'...thank you for serving us, George. Enough of this foolery! Drown him!' he commanded the creatures. Rahab pulled on his horse mask and jumped into the canal. Lilith, who was holding Mark, released her grip and dove in straight after him. Mark felt the freedom of his hands and saw this as his chance. He sprinted towards the bank and, before Oak could stop him, plunged straight into the canal and landed on the back of one of the horse figures. He was expecting to be immediately immersed in the water, passing through the creature's body as if it were smoke or fog, but instead, his elbows hit the bony back of whatever was about to pull his father down, under the dark water.

The impact of the collision shocked him, but only for half a second. In the next moment, Mark wrapped his legs around the horse's abdomen and started hammering his elbows and fists into the wildly thrashing creature's skull.

Chapter 32

Sarah

Jo came in less than fifteen minutes. In the meantime, Sarah tried to gather her strength. She knew she would need it. The storm was still raging outside, with the branches of the trees that grew near their house knocking loudly against the window of Mark's bedroom upstairs. She knew it would be hard to simply walk down the street without the wind toppling her over.

Sarah felt relieved when she heard the familiar rumble of the engine of Jo's car outside. She pushed herself to stand up, noticing that it was a little easier now. Sarah lifted her eyes to the ceiling again and whispered another prayer of thanks. She went to the door and opened it. Jo burst in, businesslike as usual.

'Are you okay? What happened to you?' she asked as she approached Sarah, doing away with the pleasantries.

'Oh, Jo! We have to find Mark and George.'

'What happened to them? Where are they in this weather?'

'I'll explain later. Please, we have to go. Help me. I need to lean on you. I don't know how long I will last.'

'Come,' Jo said, offering Sarah her shoulder to lean on as they stepped outside.

The streets had turned into brooks and streams. The water reflected the dim streetlights, windows with light in them, and occasional flashes of lightning. The rain and the darkness did not let Sarah see too far ahead.

'The canal!' Sarah said. 'They're at the canal.'

'How do you know?'

'Don't ask. Please, we must hurry.'

'What happened?' Jo asked, her face full of concern. 'Please, tell me.'

'I... I don't even know how to explain it.' She really didn't know. She didn't even realise what had actually happened. But there was one thing she had to share with her friend.

'Jo,' she said, her voice shaking as she tried to stifle a sob, 'I nearly lost the baby.'

'Oh my God!' Jo gasped. 'What happened? Did your husband... did George hit you?'

'No...' Sarah started. How was she to explain this? The door to another world – a cold, alien, lifeless, loveless world – has been smashed open, and she had just glimpsed through the doorway. 'I... I don't know what happened. George got drunk while I was away. When I came back, he became violent, but he never touched me. He shouted at me and I felt pain... pain like I'd never experienced in my life. And then I saw something. Perhaps it was my mind playing tricks on me because of the pain... It sounds totally crazy, but I saw a little girl clutching a scarlet ribbon. Her eyes were open wide in fear and I knew that if she let go of that ribbon, I'd lose her forever. And there was something else... something else pulling and twisting that ribbon. Every time the ribbon twisted, the girl screamed. And I screamed, too. Or so it seemed to me.

'Next thing I knew, Mark rushed in through the door and assaulted George. Attacked his father!'

'What?'

'Yes, I couldn't believe it either. But as soon as he did that, the little girl... kind of...' Sarah stopped, not sure how to continue. She had no words to explain what had happened.

'What happened to her, my dear?' The concern on Jo's face was genuine. This encouraged Sarah to continue.

'The little girl hugged me and... kind of melted into my body.' Sarah fell silent and the only sounds were their footsteps as they made their way down the street, towards the canals. 'And I knew from that moment that my child would be alright. It was so... so scary, Jo. And I can imagine how it sounds. Like I'm crazy or something.'

Jo put her arm around Sarah's shoulders.

'I believe you,' she said. 'There are more things in heaven and on Earth than we can imagine. And many more that we can't,' she added.

'It's frightening,' Sarah said. 'You think you know the world and then something happens and you can throw all your knowledge in the bin 'cause it turns out you know nothing.'

They walked towards the bank of the canal, as fast as Sarah's legs could carry her. Finally, they reached their destination. What they saw made both women stop in their tracks.

The water inside the canal was the colour of blood. There was a smell of rotten plants in the air.

Suddenly she heard a scream, a call for help. She recognised the voice. The desperation in it turned her blood to ice.

'Mark!' she shouted into the darkness and ran in the direction of the voice, Jo at her heels.

Chapter 33

Mark

When Mark hit the beast's back, the impact of the collision surprised not only him but also the horse. It stopped swimming towards his father but seemed to have decided to throw all its offensive strength at him instead. Mark felt the muscles in the horse's back bulge with the effort.

Suddenly, he could no longer hear his father whipping the water with his arms. All the while, he had fought for his life, thrashing and trying to shake off the hideous creature that had got to him as soon as Mark tackled the other one. Mark glanced to the side and saw the other horse holding his father under water. The beast's overalls turned into a semi-translucent pearly hide that illuminated the murky water and his father's body about a yard deep. He was still flailing his arms. He was still fighting. He was still alive.

Don't give up, Dad, Mark thought.

The creature underneath Mark began throwing itself about more wildly than ever. Mark could hardly feel his legs anymore, it was as if they had stiffened and turned into blocks of wood. He had to get off his horse and find a way to come unstuck from its back, or his strength would simply run out. He kept hammering his elbow into the point where the creature's neck connected to its skull-mask, but with each movement, his vision got darker and he moved more slowly, as if the air around him was turning into jelly.

Suddenly, he had an idea. He clutched at the creature's skull with both hands. It was the male beast, he noticed. Half of its mane was missing, with the bald patch tight around the skull, translucent like thin parchment. The slimy seaweed that covered its neck and back prevented him from getting a firm grip and he felt his hands slipping. Mark knew that if he let go, the horse would plunge towards the bottom and drag him under. He also knew what he had to do. The thought scared him, but something told him there was no other way. Finally, he closed his eyes, took a deep breath and plunged three fingers into each of the horse's dead black eyes.

The feeling was akin to sticking one's hands in liquid freezing pain. Thousands of icy needles pierced Mark's skin. He gasped in pain – just in time – and both the horse and its rider went underwater. Mark gritted his teeth: the pain in his fingers pulsated as if they had been jammed in rat-traps; then it started travelling up his arms towards his injured shoulder. It filled every cell of his flesh, piercing through the bones.

I've got to break free! I simply must!

Mark knew what he wanted to do, but the pain locked his muscles in one position, surging through him like an electric current. Finally, with one mighty effort of will, he wedged his fingers in as deep as he could, pressed the heels of his palms into the beast's skull, and pulled his arms apart.

It seemed as if he had used every single muscle in his body, every ounce of force for this final effort, and all his muscles and sinews were suddenly filled with searing pain. But the creature's skull cracked and split. Dark liquid gushed out of the crack. Mark could see grotesque black flowers blooming in the water in the light of the horse's pallid luminous hide. Then all light went out: the hide stopped glowing. Blackness consumed everything, and Mark felt freedom in his legs. He beat the water into froth, emerging towards the surface.

Breathing hurt his lungs. He gasped feverishly, not believing he was finally able to breathe in. Yet, he had another enemy to deal with. He didn't even believe the first horse (what was its name? Ray-hab?) was dead – Mark doubted that those creatures could ever be killed.

Every cell of his body screamed in protest from pain and exhaustion, but he had to dive again to try to wrestle his father from the female beast's grasp. Mark took another painful breath, braced himself and dove towards the faint light.

His father was still putting up a good fight. In the light emitted by Lilith's hide, Mark could see him trying to wrestle himself from her icy grip. Without hesitation, Mark propelled himself towards Lilith, seized her seaweed mane from behind, wrapped it around his fist and yanked her head back with all the strength he could muster. The creature let go of George and spun angrily in the water, turning towards Mark. Her slimy mane slid out of his hand, and the sharp shells that were stuck to it sliced through Mark's palm. Stinging pain filled the bleeding gashes. The eyes in Lilith's head stared unblinkingly at Mark.

Then, in an instant, the creature flung itself at him and long, black fingers like tentacles sprang from the ends of its forelimbs and wrapped themselves around Mark's neck. The creature opened its jaws full of jagged teeth, ready to sink them into his face. Before Mark could think how to react, his body responded by itself: his arm shot through the water like a torpedo and he thrust it into Lilith's throat as deep as he could. His fist went right into the creature's icy jaws; Mark grabbed at something slimy inside and twisted his fist.

He almost inhaled water: if plunging his fingers into Rahab's eye sockets had been painful, it was nothing compared to the poisonous, burning pain he was in now. In a matter of seconds, the icy stillness climbed up his arm, locking his elbow into a fixed position. He was no longer able to bend his arm, as if it was carved from a block of ice. Lilith's head and neck were immobile, but her entire body twisted and jerked frenetically. Mark gritted his teeth in pain but used his shoulder muscles to twist and pull something disgustingly cold and slimy inside the creature's throat. And then, suddenly, the jerking stopped. Lilith's hide started glowing more and more intensely, like a spotlight at a football stadium. The light made the water transparent, bringing out every object that had ever been thrown into the canal and now lay half-buried in the mud. A few yards away, he could see his father suspended in the water. He didn't move. Suddenly, the light became impossibly blinding, and the creature's skull split in two. A black and scarlet cloud erupted from the ugly crack and filled the water. Mark watched in horror as, seconds later, another cloud erupted from his father's head. The icy pain crawled up his flesh and bone towards his shoulder. He cried voicelessly, letting bubbles of air out of his mouth. Lilith's dead black eyes were fixed on him and her hide began to fade as the darkness consumed everything around.

Mark felt tension in his shoulder and realised that Lilith was sinking to the bottom, and he was going down with her. His attack had rendered him incapable of escape. He could no longer feel half of his chest, and his lungs were burning for air. Yet, any breath he would try to take would be fatal.

Lilith's hide was now hardly visible. As if from outside of his own body, Mark watched his end creep closer with each second.

He released the last bubbles of air trapped inside his lungs. *Don't breathe in. Don't breathe in!*

All light went out.

Then the water of the canal seemed to burn his hand. Before he could think, he jerked it back as if he had touched fire. The water around him was frothing as something thrashed around in it in the frenzy of a fight. Then he felt something seize the sleeve of his jacket. Instinctively, he grabbed that something, trying to struggle with it, but there was no strength in him to resist. The thing felt soft and furry. It pulled him in an unknown direction.

And out, into the air.

The air of a rather cold August night now felt soothingly warm on his face. Mark coughed and wheezed and spluttered. Next to him, snorting and spluttering, was Spot. The Labrador was growling and pulling at his sleeve. Mark groped the walls of the canal and found a rusty hold. Spot barked, let go of him and dove again.

He went for my father, Mark realised. *How does he know?*

Spot disappeared for about half a minute. Mark thought it was an eternity. Finally, he emerged. Mark rubbed his eyes, thinking he was mistaken. His father was holding Spot's collar, almost hugging his neck. He was alive, and not even unconscious. Spot snorted the water out of his nose and started barking his lungs out. Mark took it as a signal.

'Help!' he shouted, joining the dog. 'Help, anyone!'

Spot swam towards him. George was still hugging the dog's neck, not letting go.

'Dad!' Mark turned towards George. 'Are you alright?'

His father did not reply. His eyes were closing and there was no colour in his face, only sick paleness. Mark had to get help, and fast.

'Help!' he shouted again. Then he heard a response.

'Mark? Mark! Are you there?'

It was his mother.

'Mum!' Mark shouted, jerking his head back and looking upwards. He couldn't see her yet. 'Call for help. I'm here with Dad. Call the neighbours! And an ambulance.'

'Mark, I'm calling for help. Your mother will stay here.'

He recognised this voice. *Mrs Blake?*

Spot did not stop barking for a second. Mark held him and his father with one hand, gripping the iron bar with the other, but his strength was failing him. He was afraid he'd let go.

'Mum!' he shouted. 'I don't know if I can hold on any more. I need something to tie myself to. Have you got anything?'

'I've only got my coat,' the reply came.

'Tie one sleeve to the lowest iron bar you can reach and throw me the other sleeve,' Mark said. He wasn't sure it would work, but that was all he could think of. His mother did as he said, and threw the other end of the coat at him. Mark had to let go of Spot and his father for a while, otherwise he wouldn't be able to do anything.

'Spot, be a good boy and hold on to the bars,' he whispered to the dog. Surprisingly, the Labrador Retriever obeyed him and placed his front paws on the bars. Mark let go of him and spun around, grabbing at the coat. Pain shot through his entire body as he reached for the sleeve to slip his arm into it. Yet, he managed to do it, and now he hung, supported by the thick fabric that was pulled tight under his weight. He grasped Spot and his father tightly again.

'I'm all right, Mum. Thanks!' he called.

Then Mark heard the sirens. Help came. Someone brought a rope. Mark tied it around his father's chest and climbed the ladder of slippery iron bars covered in algae that were poking out of the wall of the canal, hauling his father after himself. George never let go of Spot's collar, or moved or said a word.

As soon as Mark and his father were safely on dry land, Sarah left Mrs Blake's side, rushed to them, dropped to her knees, flung her arms around them both and cried, whispering their names. George seemed to have regained consciousness and hugged her back with his free hand, breathing heavily and not saying a word.

'Mum, it's okay now,' Mark said after a few moments. 'It's okay. Please, let Dad rest. He needs it.'

The paramedics were there; they brought a stretcher and put George on it. Mark had not even noticed that the rain had subsided. The doctor unfastened Spot's collar but could not unclench Mark's father's fingers. Then he ripped at the buttons of his shirt.

'I need to check for injuries,' he explained to Mark.

'Gosh, what's this?' another doctor said, looking at the bleeding wounds on George's forearm. 'He's got dog bites here.'

Spot was sitting to one side, watching the scene attentively.

'Do you know this dog?' the doctor asked Mark. 'It may be rabid.'

'He's not rabid!' said a voice that came from behind them. Mark would have recognised this voice anywhere – low and guttural, almost like a boy's, as if damaged from constant shouting. Tandi.

'This dog has a name – Spot,' Mark said. 'He saved my dad's life tonight.'

'Mum,' he added, 'this is Tandi. That's her dog that pulled Dad out of the water.'

'He ran away,' Tandi explained, turning to Mark. 'He was so anxious, kept yelping and barking all evening. And then, as I was getting ready to go out with him, he just slipped through the door and ran away. He's never done that before. How did he know?'

'I don't know, Miss,' the paramedic said, 'but you're right, young man' he added, turning to Mark. 'This man owes his life to your dog.'

Suddenly, Mark remembered the black and scarlet cloud that had erupted from his father's cranium. He cast a worried look at his head. It was bleeding, but the doctors said it was only a skin wound, albeit an ugly one. Mark knew what had caused it – the horse's teeth.

'Your dad has suffered a shock,' the doctor said after examining him. 'He needs a lot of rest, but he's alive and that's all that matters. He's not hurt, he's just got a few scratches and small wounds here and there.

Can you tell me what happened? How did he end up in the canal?'

Mark hesitated. He did not want to lie, but there was no way he could tell the whole truth.

'He had a fight with our neighbour who pushed him into the water,' he said finally.

'Neighbour?' Mark's mother asked, raising her eyebrows.

'Oak.'

'What?' His mother's face was incredulous.

'Oak?' the doctor asked.

'That's what he calls himself,' Sarah explained to the doctor. 'Not in his right mind, that man. Imagines he's a Celtic druid or something. Where is he? And why did they fight?' she asked, turning to Mark.

'No idea. I only saw the end of it. The old man ran away after the fight. I jumped in after my dad but my clothing and shoes... I'm so lucky Spot came. Just in time.'

Suddenly Mark heard indistinct mumbling from the ground. His father had opened his eyes and his lips were moving, but Mark could not hear what he was saying.

'What is it, Dad?' Mark asked, kneeling beside him. George strained to speak for a moment. Then he raised his hand with Spot's collar in it and brought it close to his eyes. He glanced to the side and caught sight of Spot. Next, he coughed out some water, then swallowed hard and whispered:

'Good dog... Woke... me up. Good dog.'

Then he blinked. Tears started clumsily rolling down his cheeks, and for the first time in many years, he crossed himself.

'Good dog,' Mark's mother repeated. She knelt in front of Spot and planted a kiss on his black muzzle. He nudged her swelling belly with his cold nose and licked her hand.

Chapter 34

Mark

The hospital looked so clean that Mark felt his school uniform, with all that street dust on it, was as unacceptable in the ward as mucky Wellingtons would be. Mark remembered the time when he had been in hospital himself. He was barely ten back then, with a sharp and painful case of appendicitis. The conflation of scents of bleach and medicines was supposed to be the smell of cleanliness. Instead, it was the odour of foreboding, and he was happy to get out of there, to the safety of his usual world. His bed at home seemed more welcoming than ever and, as he boastfully showed the new scar in his side to the boys at school, he thought of his time in hospital as something distant, like a story in an old book.

Yet now, this jagged glass and concrete tower was the pillar upon which his hope rested. He sat down beside the only bed in the ward. Everything was so white in there – the walls, the sheets... even his father's hair. Mark looked at the face and arms of the man who seemed to be submerged in the deepest sleep. He couldn't believe this was his father – he used to look much younger six months ago. It took his hair one week to turn completely white.

'He looks like he's wearing a silver crown,' Mark's mother said to his right. 'Yes, *crown* is a suitable word,' she added. 'He's won the battle. And so have you, Mark.'

'Mum,' Mark asked for the umpteenth time, 'do you *really* believe my story? That it happened?'

He had told her everything... well, almost. He had kept the details of his conversations with Tandi to himself. Some things had to remain private. His mother looked at him. The look in her eyes was like nothing he'd seen before – or maybe he had, but was too young to remember. It was the look that spoke of a mother's heart seeing more than her eyes do.

'Of course I do,' she said. 'Of course I believe you, Mark.'

He took the risk when he decided to tell her. About the visions, about the horses, about his fight and about Oak. He thought she'd take him to the doctors. But she didn't.

This could only mean one thing: she had also seen something that night. Something that had changed her perception of reality. Mark also knew that, as a religious woman, his mother believed in the dark side as well as the good one. Had she seen a glimpse of the dark side? Or perhaps more than a glimpse? She never told him.

Mark's father suddenly smiled in his sleep. The smile brought more peace to his face. Mark and his mother seemed to feel it before they saw it, as both turned their gazes simultaneously to his father's face.

George smacked his lips in his sleep and uttered his first three sentences that morning:

'Good dog... woke me up. Thank you, Mark. Forgive me, Sarah...'

Then, as he fell back to sleep, the smile gradually left his face, but peace remained, and his slowly rising and falling chest indicated that maybe he would be all right after all.

'Good dog,' Mark heard his mother whisper. Her lips were barely moving. Then he looked back at his father. The back of his head had been carefully bandaged to conceal a torn wound that would leave an ugly scar. There was also a bandage around his left forearm. There were bite marks under that bandage. Both Mark and his mother thought that, if they could, they would order a gold medal, engrave the shape of those marks on it and hang it around the neck of the 'good dog'. George owed his life to that bite.

Sarah looked at her husband's peaceful face and placed one hand on his shoulder and the other hand on her belly, covering it protectively.

'Excuse me, Mrs Davies,' Tandi said. She was sitting nearby. Mark thought she had as much right to be there as he or his mother. His mother agreed with him. 'About your baby... Do you already know if it's a boy or a girl?'

Sarah smiled.

'It's a girl,' she said.

Mark looked at his mother's face intently. He knew what was hiding behind that smile. The lines that appeared around her eyes, those little marks of worry and sorrow... they were the tell-tale signs of what she had gone through when she fought against the world she could not really see or understand.

'How do you know?' Tandi asked. 'Have you had the scan already?'

'I just know,' his mother said simply, and Tandi understood that further questions were unnecessary. 'It's a girl. Mark will have a little sister very soon.'

'I can't wait,' Mark said, smiling. He was no longer worried. Something inside him told him that things were going to be alright after all.

'By the way, have I told you?' he said. 'I've got a job.'

'Really?' His mother turned to him with interest shining in her eyes. 'Where?'

'With a local carpenter,' Mark said. 'He makes furniture to order – just like Grandpa Chris did. He's hired me as his assistant for the rest of September – and maybe longer.'

'How did you get it?' his mother asked.

'I showed him some of the things I made out of wood,' Mark said. 'He liked them and took me on as an apprentice.'

'What about your studies?' his mother said. 'I'm not letting you forget your school work. You might make a good carpenter, but I'd like you to study for another profession, too.'

'Oh, Mrs Davies, don't worry about it,' Tandi said. 'I'll supervise him and make sure he applies himself.'

'You're a strong young woman,' Sarah said, looking at Tandi. 'Supervising Mark... I think you'll be up to the job.'

'I'm planning to go to university in the future,' Tandi said, 'and now Mark's thinking about doing that too.'

'Are you?' Sarah turned to Mark, curiosity in her eyes. 'Have you got a subject in mind?'

'I haven't thought about it that much,' Mark admitted. 'Let's get the GCSEs out of the way first.'

'All right,' his mother said with a smile. 'You do that.'

The door to the ward opened. A middle-aged doctor stepped in and greeted them all. Mark's mother stood up.

'How is he, doctor?' she asked with anxiety in her voice.

'Getting better,' the doctor replied. 'We'll discharge him soon enough. But he needs plenty of rest. A month or two off work — we could arrange sick leave for him. He is totally exhausted.'

'But will he be okay?' Mark heard his mother ask.

'He will,' the doctor assured. 'Just let him sleep. Sleep is the best medicine he could get now.'

*

Mark's father was discharged from the hospital two weeks after school had started. He stayed at home, resting and spending time with his family. There was plenty to catch up with.

Right up until the end of September, Mark went to work at the local carpenter's shop every day. From the start of October, he would only go there in the evening a couple of days a week and at the weekends. In the evenings, he would usually either meet Tandi or stay at home, talking to his parents. Tandi insisted that he do more of the latter.

In the last weekend of September, Mark and Tandi decided to go to Sarehole Mill. They sat on the bank of the River Cole and ate sandwiches prepared by Mark's mother, enjoying what they thought to be the last warm days of the year.

Mark didn't feel like broaching the subject, but he felt he had to.

'Do you think they'll come back?'

Tandi knew what he was talking about.

'I don't know,' she said. 'Do you think they're dead?'

'I don't believe they can die. Do you?'

'No,' Tandi said, shaking her head. 'And Oak?'

'He's nowhere to be seen. I'm not surprised. He's shown his true colours and wouldn't come back.'

'But they're somewhere else, making someone else's life a misery.'

Mark nodded. Sadly, that was most probably the case.

'All we can do now is pray that as few people as possible meet them,' he said.

'Do you think there are a lot of people like us?' Tandi asked. 'People who can see them?'

'I'm afraid so,' Mark said. 'We can't be the only ones. But I hope I never see them again.'

He wasn't sure how, but Mark knew both of them were thinking about the same thing: something special united them now that they had seen what they had seen. Something that was very hard to break. That thought made Mark happy.

'How's your dad?' Tandi asked, changing the subject.

'Much better,' Mark said. 'He can't wait to get back to work. He's already doing DIY around the house. It's what he likes.'

'And your mum? When's she due?'

'End of January.'

'You're going to have a little sister.'

'Yeah,' Mark said. He was getting impatient now. He still remembered her little face from that day. He was certain this was what she'd look like.

'I like your family,' Tandi said. 'They seem like a nice bunch. Especially some members,' she added with a cheeky smile.

'You don't say,' Mark replied with the same smile. 'I haven't had a chance to meet yours yet, by the way.'

'You're right. I'd like you to meet my auntie. She's been asking about you.'

'You've told her about me?'

'Of course I have. She said you sound like a nice young man. I agree with her.'

Mark felt heat rise in his face. He was blushing.

'You look like a tomato now!' Tandi said, bursting into laughter.

'A very pleased tomato, though,' Mark replied, grinning.

She bent towards him and kissed him.

Chapter 35

Epilogue

People travel and stories travel with them. Sometimes, stories become real. They live on, after the storytellers have departed.

Some stories come from one person's imagination. Such was the story of Sarah Davies and Mary Beth. The night Sarah almost lost her baby, she thought of Jo Blake, not Mary Beth. That was the night when Mary Beth's story ended. Imaginary friends cannot come to help you. Real friends can.

Some stories are older than that. They live in old caves and streams and lakes. They can also come to live in modern cities like Birmingham. The story of the Kelpie, a mysterious shape-shifting water horse that drowns its rider, has come from the Scottish Highlands to the West Midlands, from the million-year-old underwater caves around lochs to the brick tunnels over the canals.

Mark Davies knows that story. So does Tandi Bryce. But it's a story they will not tell their children. Both believe that it is better this way – some stories should not be told; some characters should not outlive the storyteller.

People travel, and so do their stories. Many stories are born out of loneliness and isolation. These are the most dangerous stories, because they are more tempting than the real world. People forget to live and trap themselves inside the story. Such was the story of George Davies and Rahab, the beast whose existence is prolonged by two purposes – lies and murder. Stories born out loneliness never end well. Once you become a character in such a story, there is no way out. George was able to escape only because he was not alone.

To be lonely is to live in a prison that you have built with your own hands. It's the most secure prison in the world. And soon, you will discover that you are not as lonely as you thought – company will appear. More Rahabs and more Liliths. More lies and more murder.

THE END

About the Author

Roy Eynhallow is a writer of supernatural fiction and urban fantasy. He is sharing his writing journey through his blog at

www.HallowBooks.com.

He is currently exploring the mysterious side of the city of Birmingham, England.

You can find Roy on Facebook. His page is called **'Roy Eynhallow, Writer.'**

And on Twitter **@EynhallowBooks**.

Finally, you can email your questions and comments to **roy.eynhallow@gmail.com**.

Author's note:

Thank you very much for reading my book! If you liked it, please leave a review on Amazon. If there is anything that you did not like, or if you found any mistakes in the book, you can contact me and tell me about it. I'm sure I can fix them!

Thank you in advance.

Roy Eynhallow

Made in the USA
Charleston, SC
09 May 2016